Reaso~~nable~~

and

Necessary

Other books by John D. Mills:

The Manatee Murders
The Objector
Sworn Jury
The Trophy Wife Divorce
The Hooker, the Dancer and the Nun

Reasonable
and
Necessary

by

John D. Mills

Pono

www.PonoPubs.com

Library of Congress Control Number: TBA

ISBN -13: 978-1519426291
ISBN -10: 1519426291

Printed in the United States
Second Edition

Editor: Megan Parker, Calliope & Quill
Layout and editing: Inge Heyer

Cover art and map of Pine Island Sound: Cameron Graphics

Pono Publishing
Laramie, Wyoming
Hilo, Hawai`i

www.PonoPubs.com

Acknowledgements

I am very grateful to the following people that read my original manuscript and offered ideas for improvement:

Professor Russell Franklin
JoEllen Kane
Amy Anthony
Doug Wilkinson
Cathy Lucrezi
Bruce Oliphant
Gail Lawson
Jay Meisenberg
Wendy Resh
John Shearer
Leslie Stoddard
Carmen Dellutri
Joy Mills
Dick Ackert
Lisa Fasig
Megan Parker
Stephanie J. Slater
Timothy F. Slater
Inge Heyer

Cabbage Key is a special place, and we can all thank Rob and Phyllis Wells and their friendly staff for a little piece of heaven in southwest Florida.

Pine Island

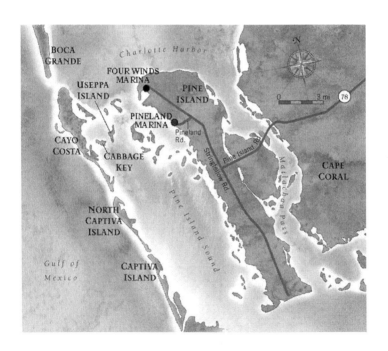

Pine Island is the largest island off Florida's Gulf Coast,
located in Lee County in southwest Florida.

Chapter 1

"Who the hell is Ginger Smith? And why did you help her buy a red Porsche identical to yours?" Sarah Elsworth screamed as her husband, Dr. Chadwick "Chad" Elsworth III, walked in the door after work.

Chad's stomach churned with acid as he quickly processed his situation. He didn't know how much she knew, so he decided to buy time while he developed a strategy.

"She's a nurse at the hospital," Chad replied slowly as he analyzed his wife's face to see if she believed him. "She admired my Porsche and asked me to help her get a fair price at the dealership. Why are you so angry?"

Sarah screamed in a piercing voice, "The service manager from the dealership called and said the tint job was done on my new Porsche. When I told them we don't have a new Porsche, he said he saw you buy the Porsche last week with your wife! I drove to the dealership and found out it's owned by a Ginger Smith. Everybody got real quiet at the dealership. Is she your girlfriend?"

Chad silently cursed the manager as he slowly grinned at his wife. His face turned pale and he spoke in his best bedside manner voice, "Honey, she's a friend from work. She inherited some money and wanted a Porsche, so she asked me to help her buy it so the salesmen wouldn't rip her off."

Sarah yelled, "You're full of shit, Chad. You're no humanitarian unless she has big boobs and a nice ass! How long have you been fucking her?"

The doorbell rang and gave Chad a chance to gather his thoughts about the lie over his girlfriend's Porsche.

"You're overreacting, Sarah. She's a friend, and that's all." While walking over to the door, Chad's gait was more like a young Ichabod Crane than the college athlete he was a decade before.

"My friends warned me about you, but I wouldn't listen. You are a fucking asshole!" Sarah said through tears. Her wrinkles seemed to be deepening every time she looked in the mirror.

Chad answered the front door and was shocked to see a sheriff's deputy. He wondered if one of his nosy neighbors had called the cops because of the yelling.

The deputy asked boldly, "Are you Dr. Chadwick Elsworth III ?"

"Yes, I am," Chad answered quietly. "What have I done?"

"You are served. A lawsuit has been filed against you, Dr. Elsworth, and I hope you have good insurance."

Chad took the complaint and went to his family room

to read it. As Sarah cried quietly on the couch and watched the latest scandal on the evening news, he read the medical malpractice lawsuit the Martin family had filed against him for 15 million dollars because of the death of Bobby Martin. He saw that Karen Senard was the lawyer and recalled she had successfully sued three of his doctor friends for medical malpractice.

Chad became light-headed, and his breathing was labored. The room seemed to shrink and slowly started to turn counter-clockwise as he remembered he had no malpractice insurance—he'd used the premium payment as the down payment on Ginger's Porsche.

Chad sat in a daze in his leather recliner and didn't respond to Sarah's questions. After 10 minutes of silence, she walked over to him and picked up the lawsuit he'd dropped on the floor. She read the complaint while standing over him and asked what it was about. Chad ignored her until she finally went into the kitchen and called her mother. He could imagine his mother-in-law criticizing him once again because it seemed to be her favorite pastime. He felt unsteady as he stood up and drifted over to the wet bar and poured himself a glass of Dewar's scotch. It was the first of many.

*   *   *   *   *

The next morning Chad woke up with a world-class

hangover and a sore back. He'd fallen asleep in his recliner watching *Star Trek* reruns. He stumbled into the bathroom and washed his face with cold water as he slowly remembered the fight he and Sarah had before he'd passed out. He drifted into the kitchen and tried to make a sausage omelet, but threw up while mixing the eggs. He cleaned up and made coffee while he read the morning paper.

As he drank his morning coffee, he felt it mixing with the remaining bile in his stomach. He avoided throwing up by walking outside for fresh air. The cool late spring morning made him shiver. His dog, Bud, a black lab, had treed a squirrel and was barking. Chad thought that the barking seemed much louder than normal in his vulnerable state. He silently wished he had the same life as a dog; if you can't eat it or screw it, piss on it.

Chad called his office and told them he was sick. He told his staff to call his patients to reschedule their appointments. He then called his friend, Dr. Charles "Trip" Cleland III and arranged for golf after they had a martini lunch. Chad always solved his hangover by drinking the following day. They met at the Dunwoody Country Club for lunch at the bar, where they watched the noon edition of ESPN Sports Center while debating whether the Braves would make the World Series. After three martinis they walked out of the clubhouse and loaded up their golf cart. While they were playing golf, Chad confided in Trip about the lawsuit and

4

Ginger's Porsche.

"You didn't pay your malpractice premium. Holy shit! This could put you in bankruptcy court, and Sarah will freak out if she loses her Mercedes. No wonder you got drunk last night," Trip said sympathetically to his friend.

"Tell me something I don't know. This isn't fair; the goddamn HMO, LAMPCO, wouldn't approve the MRI. That would've showed the tumor, and we could've treated it. It's their fault Bobby Martin died. They should have to pay!" Chad screamed across the fairway on the third hole.

After a few seconds of uncomfortable silence, Trip stated coldly, "If you blame LAMPCO, you'll be blackballed and lose all of the HMO business. If you don't blame LAMPCO, you'll have a 15 million judgment against you personally, and you'll lose everything. Basically, you have no way out."

Chad three-putted the hole and didn't even care. His life was falling apart. Everything he had worked for was slipping through his fingers. He didn't know what to do, except have another beer with his afternoon amphetamine. The energy boost helped him hit the ball farther.

After playing two more holes in silence, Trip suddenly said, "Fast Eddie. You need Fast Eddie."

Chad took a deep breath and nodded slowly.

*   *   *   *   *

Fast Eddie's full name was Edward Rankin Palsky. He was a seasoned lawyer that had made a good living working on high profile media cases. He tried to settle injury cases as fast as possible, even though it might be to his client's detriment. Eddie just wanted his one-third contingency fee ASAP. No one was faster to be retained on a high profile case and settle when there was a contingency fee available. The free advertising from the media coverage had allowed Eddie's practice to grow at the expense of his professional reputation. He was an outcast among the local Atlanta Bar members because of his tactics.

Fast Eddie's most recent case had raised a few eyebrows in Atlanta. Senator Butch Thormon had died at 98. He wanted his remains cremated and spread on the eighteenth green at the Old South Country Club in Griffin, Georgia. The Old South Country Club was a private club that had the dubious distinction of being the last "white only" country club in Georgia. One month after the Senator's supposed remains were spread on the eighteenth green, Mike Lee, an Asian worker at the Griffin funeral home, gave an interview to *The Washington Post*.

Mr. Lee had switched the Senator's cremated remains with Willie Jones, a black homeless man who died of AIDS. Mr. Lee had thought Senator Thormon was a bigot and thought it would be a funny joke.

The Old South Country Club was very embarrassed.

6

They consulted with the Senator's family and decided to burn the eighteenth green and create a new green adjacent to the old green. They renamed the eighteenth hole as The Senator Thormon Memorial Hole.

Fast Eddie looked up the survivors of Willie Jones and solicited them as clients. On the day the new eighteenth green was being dedicated, Fast Eddie filed a lawsuit against the Old South Country Club for grave desecration and racial discrimination. He had a press conference at his office to condemn the actions of the Old South Country Club. Fast Eddie was pleased that he made *CNN* that night. True to form, he settled with the club the next day for $50,000.

Chad knew he needed a good lawyer that was not afraid to buck the system. Fast.

Eddie was exactly the man for the job. As soon as he finished the round of golf, Chad called Fast Eddie's office for an appointment.

Chapter 2

Karen Lynn Senard was born in Hawkinsville, Georgia in 1960. Her father was a lumber worker at the local paper mill and her mother a secretary until she died while Karen was in college. Karen was an only child, and her parents encouraged her to participate in extracurricular activities to improve her social skills. During high school she played the saxophone in the marching band and played volleyball.

She decided she wanted to be a lawyer when she was in her early teens. A large national chemical company had been blamed for pollution in her local water supply. The unsafe chemicals in the fertilizers purchased by the local farmers had contaminated the local lakes and the large companies refused to admit responsibility. A sole practitioner in Hawkinsville, Jay Hall, had represented the local farmers. The chemical company brought in lawyers from Philadelphia, New York, and Atlanta to defend the suit.

The two-month trial took place in federal court in Macon. The jury ruled in favor of the local plaintiffs and awarded 10 million dollars for injuries and cleanup of the water supply.

Karen wanted to be able to help the little people. She imagined herself to be a modern day Robin Hood. After the success of her hero, Jay Hall, she knew what she wanted to do. Every summer she worked in his office as a runner. She watched in admiration as he helped average workers successfully battle large insurance companies. All of Mr. Hall's clients were very grateful for the help and told all of their families and friends what a fine man he was.

Karen was a very focused student while growing up in Hawkinsville. She enjoyed the social activities in high school, but did not date. She saw how many of her girl-friends were more concerned with boys than school. She decided she was not going to let any boys interfere with her plans to be a big-time lawyer. Karen had raven black hair that contrasted with her fair skin. She had been a tall, lanky girl until ninth grade when her hormones went into overdrive and started producing womanly curves. She tried to hide her developing figure by wearing oversized sweaters and baggy pants.

While in high school, Karen worked at the local Dairy Queen on weekends for spending money. Her Dairy Queen T-shirts and jeans caused many local boys to have continuous cravings for ice cream. She had many admiring boys ask her out for dates, but she never went because she didn't want anything to get in the way of her goal of going to law school. She also created an incentive system for herself;

there would be no local farm boys in her love life because she was going to wait for college and meet a more mature man.

Karen excelled at volleyball and earned an athletic scholarship to Mercer University in Macon, Georgia. She was thrilled to go to college and get out of Hawkinsville. Even though Mercer University was only an hour away from home, it was a whole different world. Students were smarter, classes larger, tests harder, and college men more interesting.

Karen learned a lot about dating from her girlfriends in her dormitory. It bothered her that many of them were on emotional roller coasters when it came to their sex lives. A lot of Karen's friends happily lost their virginity in their first semester at college. They enjoyed their sex lives until the breakup with their first lover. The girls became hysterical, trying anything to hold onto their first love.

She sensed these boyfriends knew they had this power over their conquered women and felt they treated them badly in many cases. Some girls felt terribly guilty about losing their virginity while other girls were quick to move on to different men. Karen listened to both type of girls complaining about the power they felt their first lover had over them.

Karen began dating in her freshman year. She had a few close experiences, but was still a virgin after her freshman year. She made straight A's and was at the top of her class. She decided to take advantage of her scholarship and go

11

to summer school. It was definitely better than working at Dairy Queen and having farm boys stare at her.

That summer Karen decided that she was ready to experience sex. She knew because of the focus on her career that she would never marry the first man she had sex with. She also knew that she did not want any man having control over her emotionally because he had taken her virginity. One night after reading *Playgirl*, she figured out the solution to her dilemma. She read that 95% of men take their virginity without the benefit of a partner. Maybe she could take her own virginity, she thought. If a man could do it, so could she.

The next afternoon she put on dark sunglasses, a hat, and old clothes and drove her faded gray Honda Accord to an adult toy store in downtown Macon. It was an older section of downtown that had many out-of-business stores in the two-story buildings. Some buildings had apartments on the top level. Karen looked up to the windows and saw sad, empty faces looking through the dusty glass.

Karen pulled into a parking space near *Delilah's Den*, where she sat in her car for 20 minutes before she got enough courage to go inside. She looked to see if any one she knew was in the store or walking down the street. She was amazed at all the new Porsches parked in front of *Delilah's Den*.

Karen entered *Delilah's Den* and was greeted by the

12

distinctive smell of cinnamon candles burning and the stereo quietly playing Otis Redding's "Sitting by the Dock of the Bay." The walls were painted bright pink, and a poster of Tom Cruise hung over the dressing room. Although nervous, she became more comfortable when she looked around and saw everyone intensely browsing. A saleslady asked if she could help, but Karen said she was just looking; she was too embarrassed to ask for the vibrator section, so she looked through the store until she found it. Some items amused her, some confused her, and some scared her. After two hours of debating, she picked her battery powered first love.

She stopped at Flaming Sally's Liquor Store on the way back to her dorm and got a bottle of Chablis. Back at her dorm's parking lot, she put the wine and her new toy in a duffel bag, walked quickly to her room, double locked the door, and put on James Taylor's Greatest Hits. She began drinking the wine and debating her decision. The good side was there was no chance for sexually transmitted disease. The bad side was she could never again listen to "Sweet Baby James" without laughing.

After Karen finished the bottle of wine, she decided that she had gotten her date drunk enough. She put an old blue towel on her bed and laid down on it. She then thought of her favorite love scene from *An Officer and a Gentleman*. After it was over, Karen felt relaxed and relieved. While she showered, she began thinking of men in a different way and

13

was certain she would enjoy her new hobby.

The next morning while walking away from the class-rooms in the old chapel, Karen saw the cute guy that had been staring at her for the past week in English Literature class. She caught his eye and said energetically, "Hi, my name is Karen."

"Hi, my name is Alan. What do you think of our professor?" Alan Leopart nervously replied.

Karen smiled. "I think she likes to hear herself talk. She probably watches herself lecture in the mirror at home."

Alan looked around cautiously and then quipped, "All of her mirrors must be cracked a hundred times."

Karen and Alan laughed at each other's jokes, and they both felt a rush of blood to their faces. They talked for a few minutes and then decided to have lunch together. Alan was a year older than Karen with a medium build and light brown hair. His dark brown eyes conveyed a strong sense of intelligence. He hadn't met Karen before because he was an education major and involved in a fraternity, which took most of his spare time.

Karen played in volleyball and studied long hours during the normal school year. However, during summer school things were different. The professors just wanted to earn a little extra money and didn't take the time to draft long assignments or give tests that were difficult to grade. Therefore, the academic pressure of summer school was minimal.

Because of no fraternity activities or volleyball practice during summer school, Karen and Alan found they had
more free time. Their romance blossomed, and they began
their sexual relationship two weeks after they began dating.
It was a magical time for them because it was the first hot
and heavy romance for either one. The limited number of
students and the relaxed grading standards, coupled with the
perfect romance, was intoxicating to both of them.

After final exams for summer school were over, Alan
went to Karen's dorm room and invited her for dinner at the
Veranda, the nicest restaurant in Macon. Karen was impressed, but asked, "How are you going to pay for it?"

"My grandparents sent me some money for my birthday.
I can't think of anything else I'd rather spend it on," Alan
said sincerely.

Karen smiled and had to cross her legs because of the
warm feeling that came over her.

"What time?" She asked.

"Eight. I'll see you then," Alan said as he walked toward the door.

Karen jumped up, stepped in front of him, quietly locked
her door, and said, "Appetizers are served now!"

After a vigorous afternoon together, Alan and Karen
were starved. They had a bottle of the house champagne
during their lobster dinner. The piano player at the baby
grand played classical music during dinner. It was the first

time they had ever had champagne together and Karen wondered what the special occasion was.

After dinner, Alan handed Karen an envelope. She opened the envelope and found a typed poem, which she read to herself.

The Quest
As a child, I saw my Dad,
but before we would play,
he hugged my mother and would say,
"I love you more every day."

As a boy, I watched movies and T.V.
The leading man would always get the girl,
He would profess his love with the greatest of ease,
They always fit like an oyster and a pearl.

As a teenager, I became a skeptic of the perfect match,
I saw others use the word "love" as a tool.
Some would say, "He's the perfect catch."
Others would say, "He's such a fool."

As a young man, I have met you.
I now know why men say, "I do."
Violets may be blue; Roses may be red,
But I want you to wake up every morning, in my bed.

Karen wiped away her tears and asked tentatively, "What do you mean by this? It's beautiful, but what do you mean?"

Alan poured out his heart. "I want you to marry me. Not now, because I can't afford a ring, but I want you to know."

They both agreed that it was too soon. Karen was overwhelmed and confused with her feelings. She didn't tell Alan, but she hadn't planned on getting married until she was at least thirty, after her career was established.

Karen thought it was a nice feeling to be in love, but marriage was out of the question. She was afraid to tell Alan she wanted to wait until she was thirty, but she reasoned that since Alan said he wanted to wait, and she wanted to wait, why did they have to discuss how long? She thought her logic would make a lawyer proud.

After classes started back in the fall, Karen and Alan continued to date. However, their different friends and activities returned. They got into the habit of studying together during the week, going back to her dorm room, having sex, and going to sleep. Karen thrived under this situation. She was happy socially and continued her straight A's. Alan wanted them to get an apartment together and live off campus. He said if he quit his fraternity, he could afford off-campus housing. Karen lied and said her mother wouldn't approve, but she wanted Alan to keep busy with his fraternity because he was starting to take too much of her time.

During the winter of her sophomore year, Karen's mother went to her doctor with a complaint of dizziness and pain in her lower back. The doctor ran some tests in his office and concluded it was muscle spasm because of over-exertion. The pain continued over the next few months and she returned to the doctor three times, but he only prescribed painkillers and muscle relaxants. The pain increased and ultimately one Sunday afternoon Karen's father drove her to the hospital. The emergency room doctor examined her and ordered more tests after reviewing the CAT scans. Later Sunday night, a serious and somber chief surgeon of the hospital broke the news to Karen and her father.

A cancerous ovarian cyst had grown and spread through her entire stomach area. No surgery could remove it because of its advanced stage. She only had days to live, but they would give her morphine to ease the pain. When the chief surgeon was told of the medical treatment she had received over the past six months, he was shocked and then angry. He gave them the name of an attorney that specialized in medical malpractice.

Two weeks after Karen's mother died, they consulted with the attorney. They were outraged to learn that their original doctor had been sued 12 times over the past five years because of malpractice. The medical experts for Karen's family agreed that it was a terrible case of misdiagnosis. The doctor didn't order any advanced tests because he had lost his hospital privileges two years before. Karen's father received a settlement that he later used to pay for Karen's law school education. Because Karen and her father were devastated by her mother's sudden death, she decided to spend time in Hawkinsville with her father that summer. She knew from that point on she wanted to be an attorney for victims of medical malpractice.

While she was away from Alan, she started to think of the emotional attachment she was forming with him. He wanted to marry and start a family immediately, which distracted her focus on her studies. The more she thought about, the more it bothered her. She decided to break the emotional bond she had formed with Alan. Over the summer, Karen looked up three of her former admirers from high school, and the muscular farm boys finally got their wish with Karen.

When Karen returned to Mercer in the fall, she told Alan that they should date other people. Alan was devastated, but Karen didn't want her feelings for Alan to affect her plans for law school and her career. There'd be time for love when she was secure in her career, she told herself.

From her junior year on, Karen always had a regular boyfriend. Some only lasted a month, others six months. Some broke up with her and that was okay with her. Karen always broke up when they started getting serious. Karen's motto was she didn't want to date men who used four letter words—like "love" and "ring."

In between boyfriends Karen would call Alan late at night because she knew that he was still in love with her. She enjoyed his affections but wouldn't allow herself to open up emotionally. Karen studied hard, enjoyed men's company when she had time, and went to sleep. She kept her emotions in control because no man was going to spoil her goal.

Her disciplined lifestyle in college earned her straight A's. She continued her same pattern at the Walter F. George School of Law at Mercer. When she graduated, her first job was with a big firm in Atlanta working in defense of medical malpractice. She shrewdly calculated that she could learn all the tricks defending doctors and then use it against them at a later date.

The last time she saw Alan was when she was in Macon for a case. Her firm was defending a doctor that had given the wrong medication to a man who died. Alan was teaching school in Macon and Karen called him. They agreed to meet at the *Veranda* for dinner.

When Karen walked into the restaurant, Alan rushed up to her and said, "You look great. It's been two years, but you look even better."

Karen said, "Thank you, you look good yourself. I'm starved, let's eat."

Alan had previously arranged for the hostess to seat them at the table where he had proposed eight years previously. After they had finished dinner, Alan asked, "Do you remember the last time we sat at this table?"

Karen had hoped it was just a coincidence and Alan wouldn't open up his old wounds. Karen replied politely, "I remember, it was sweet. But it's been a long time."

Alan was embarrassed and said, "I know it's been a long time. But I've always felt something special for you, Karen. I was glad you called me for dinner because I've been thinking about you lately. I've been seeing someone for about 18 months, and I was seriously thinking of marriage. But ... I always think about you and wonder who you're dating. Are you seeing anyone?"

Karen thought quickly and lied, "Yes, I've been seeing this neurosurgeon pretty seriously."

Alan quickly retreated and decided to save face, "I'm glad for you. I'm happy and hope you are too."

They finished their drinks over polite conversation about mutual friends. Alan walked Karen to her car and they shook hands.

Karen had gotten three other marriage proposals over the years, and she turned all of them down. All of the men had far too large of egos; she didn't want a male chauvinist as a husband. She had male friends to call when she felt the need for affection. If not for her biological clock, Karen would've been happy with her life.

After three years of defending doctors, she opened her own firm representing victims of medical malpractice. She prospered because of her knowledge and her own passion for understanding the pain of her clients.

Karen listened intently to the Martin family when they came to her office. She told them how she lost her mother, and they connected. Karen was going to do everything she could to make Dr. Chadwick Elsworth III pay for his mistake.

Chapter 3

Bobby Martin was an idealistic man who believed if you worked hard and took care of your family, God would take care of you. Born and raised in Dalton, Georgia, he enlisted in the army at 18 and served three years in Vietnam. After he was honorably discharged, he came back home and married his high school sweetheart, Mary. They moved to Atlanta because of the job market, and he was hired by Amex Tools and advanced with the company because of his excellent work. They had three girls within their first five years of marriage.

Bobby was at his 47th birthday party when he first noticed the pain in his left side. Like most men of his generation, he ignored the pain until it went away. However, it came back the next day. He confided in his wife about it while eating his breakfast of whole wheat toast, no butter, and prune juice.

"Dr. Elsworth is the internist on your insurance plan. I'll call and make an appointment tomorrow," Mary informed Bobby.

"It's probably all of that low-fat cooking you've been

doin'. If God meant for us to eat low-fat, he wouldn't have given us taste buds," Bobby complained as he forced the prune juice down. When he left for work, he made his daily stop at the McDonald's drive-through for his favorite sausage biscuit.

Bobby went to see Dr. Elsworth the next day who did a physical exam and interviewed Bobby about his medical history. He had the nurse do a blood draw in the examination room while he called Bobby's insurance company, LAMPCO, for approval of an MRI from his office.

"No, Dr. Elsworth, we cannot approve the MRI at this time," said the authorization technician who took the call.

"Why? This patient is having severe pain, and I need to find the cause. The MRI is the best tool to make this determination. I need to talk to someone else above you. This is ridiculous; put your supervisor on the phone."

Chad began seething as he held 10 minutes waiting for the insurance adjuster, with a business degree, to tell him how to practice medicine. He became angrier by the minute.

"Dr. Elsworth, this is Matt Dagan, I'm in charge of this department. How can I help you?"

Dr. Elsworth went through a 15-minute explanation of why Bobby needed an MRI. At the end of the explanation, he added that he had trouble before with LAMPCO denying MRI tests for other patients.

"Yes, Dr. Elsworth, I agree that you've complained before about our company. My computer shows that you filed for five formal reviews for patients in the past six months. All were denied by our expert. My computer also shows that I have four other internists in your area that want to be on our plan. Perhaps you can withdraw from our plan if you're not happy with our service."

"What does it take for you people to approve an MRI?" Chad yelled into the phone.

"Our expert tells us a MRI is only justified when other tests show an objective need for it. Our plan only pays for medical treatment that is reasonable and necessary," Matt Dagan repeated for the twentieth time that morning.

"But it might be too late after other tests show the need," Chad pleaded.

"Dr. Elsworth, the answer is no. If you don't want our business, we can take you off our plan."

Chad thought for a couple of seconds of all his outstanding financial obligations and his girlfriend's new Porsche that he was paying for. "No. No, I want to be on your plan. I'll do other tests."

"Have a good day, Dr. Elsworth," Matt Dagan concluded triumphantly.

LAMPCO had just denied their twentieth MRI request for the morning. Matt Dagan figured at $1,500 a piece, he just made his company an additional $30,000 that morning.

Chad returned to the examination room and told Bobby,

"I'll let you know after the blood tests come back. We may not need an MRI."

"I thought you wanted to do an MRI test," Bobby said, "I'm a firm believer in doing what the doctor orders."

Chad lied to Bobby, "We'll wait until after the blood work."

Bobby came back a month later to Dr. Elsworth, complaining about the pain in his side. The x-rays and blood work didn't show anything wrong. Chad didn't order an MRI because he knew LAMPCO wouldn't approve it. He also didn't want to risk upsetting the managers at LAMPCO and possibly losing a source of business. Chad gave Bobby a prescription for excess stomach acid.

Six months later, Bobby and Mary were vacationing in the North Carolina Mountains. Bobby was driving along a winding road when he blacked out and ran into the ditch. Mary wasn't hurt in the accident, but Bobby was taken to the hospital because he was unconscious. In the emergency room, Dr. Anthony ordered an MRI to check for a collapsed lung.

The MRI showed an unnatural growth in Bobby's left kidney.

Dr. Anthony reluctantly reported to Bobby's wife, "Mrs. Martin, I have good news and bad news. The good news is that your husband doesn't have a collapsed lung. The bad news is that he has a tumor in his left kidney the size of a grapefruit."

Mary collapsed into her seat in shock and confusion.

"My husband saw a doctor in Atlanta twice about the pain in his left side. He said it was stomach acid."

Dr. Anthony explained how they were running more tests to diagnose the tumor.

Chapter 4

"Civil RICO. What is that?" Chad asked Fast Eddie.

"RICO stands for Racketeer Influenced and Corrupt Organizations. Prosecutors use it in criminal court to go after organizations that show a pattern of criminal actions. However, Georgia is one of a few states that allows a private citizen to sue a person, or a corporation, in civil court for organized criminal activity. If the suit is successful, a plaintiff can collect triple damages and attorney fees," Fast Eddie stated while he simultaneously was mentally calculating his potential attorney fees for such a case. He sat back in his chair at his desk and looked across his desk at his bewildered client.

"I don't understand. I've been sued by the Martin family. How do I show LAMPCO was the cause of the suit?" Chad asked.

Fast Eddie leaned forward and smiled mischievously. "You file a third-party lawsuit against LAMPCO, alleging civil RICO. You'll allege that LAMPCO is an organization involved in a criminal enterprise, theft, and they have a pattern of conduct of denying MRI's for claimants. The allegation of theft is that LAMPCO takes in premiums with the promise to pay for reasonable and necessary medical treatments when they know they won't pay for valid treatment. We can also claim that LAMPCO attracts customers by falsely advertising it is dedicated to quality medical care, when in fact, the company encourages system-wide cost-cutting undermining quality care.

"LAMPCO will go ballistic because they don't want their claims procedures exposed. Once Karen Senard realizes that you have no malpractice insurance, she'll want to find a deep pocket. If she gets a 15 million-dollar judgment against you and you have no insurance, she knows you'll file bankruptcy and she won't get nothin'. She'll go after LAMPCO for not approving the MRI tests and you'll testify for her."

Chad shook his head and said quietly, "If I blame the HMO, I'm going to be blackballed by the other insurance companies, and I'll go out of business."

Fast Eddie shrugged and said matter-of-factly, "If you don't blame the HMO, you'll be bankrupt and out of business because Karen Senard will make sure every newspaper and TV station knows of her big verdict against you. She's almost a bigger media hound than me."

Chad's world was collapsing. He had told Ginger about his wife finding out about the Porsche, and she seemed bothered that he lied to his wife about their relationship. Chad explained to her about the malpractice suit and his lack of insurance, while Ginger scolded him about his lack of financial planning. Ginger suddenly developed PMS for the first time in their six-month relationship and said she just needed some time alone.

Chad was getting tired of sleeping on the couch at night. He continued to deny the affair to Sarah, but he could tell she didn't believe him, and she told him constantly. Sarah's father called him daily to inquire about the malpractice lawsuit and how he was going to handle it. He could always hear his mother-in-law in the background complaining about how irresponsible he was.

Chad said wearily to Fast Eddie, "I don't know, I just don't know. Tell me what you would do. I can't think clearly, that's why I'm paying you."

Fast Eddie leaned back in his chair and put his hands behind his head. "When you bring the third-party lawsuit against LAMPCO, they'll fold. They will pay off the malpractice claim and have the Martin family agree to a confidentiality clause because they don't want their claim practices exposed. They also don't want to risk triple damages and attorney fees against 'em. I don't want to pat myself on the back, but they don't want to risk me making a media circus with the case either."

Chad weighed his options and finally realized there was no other way out. He knew he committed malpractice by not ordering the MRI. He'd have to file bankruptcy if he lost the lawsuit, and it was not fair because LAMPCO was to blame. He looked over at Fast Eddie and debated with himself whether this short, pock-faced lawyer with his Vitalis-slicked hair should be trusted.

After a short hesitation, Chad looked Fast Eddie in the eyes and said defiantly, "Do it! Sue the bastards."

"You're doing the right thing, Dr. Elsworth. I need a retainer fee of $25,000 to get started, and I bill at $300 per hour," Fast Eddie explained in his best bedside manner.

Chapter 5

Downtown Atlanta was deserted at 8:00 a.m. on a drizzling, Saturday morning, so Karen was able to park her Red Saab directly in front of Peachtree Towers. She took the elevator to her office on the eighth floor. When she opened the mahogany door, she saw her paralegal, Jamie McDaniel, in her wheelchair working at her computer.

Jamie looked over her computer and said, "It's eight in the morning. What are ya doing here, boss? Wasn't your new boyfriend worth sleeping in for?"

Karen replied, "We got into a fight last night and he went home. Tim is a nice guy, and if he didn't bother me about working so much, we'd get along better. Last night, he reminded me I wasn't getting any younger if I wanted to have children. He knows how to push my buttons, so I told him to leave. I think I'm gonna take your advice and get one big and dumb."

"If you find one, ask if he has a friend. The nights have been getting cold lately," Jamie answered quietly.

Karen lamented, "Every time I get in a fight with a new boyfriend, I think back to college and remember Alan. He's married now with two kids. Why are all the good ones taken?"

"I'm really tired of ya talking about Alan. Ya need to find a new story," Jamie laughingly scolded.

Karen slowly nodded her head and said, "I know. Things were so simple then, and I miss it."

Karen took her mail from the receptionist desk and walked back to her office. She enjoyed her quiet Saturday mornings at the office. She was able to concentrate on her work without the interruption of phone calls, court hearings, or unscheduled clients with repetitive questions.

Jamie was Karen's trusted paralegal of eight years. Jamie had worked at Northern Trust Casualty for 10 years as a claims adjuster before she had taken the paralegal job with Karen's office. While at Northern Trust, she had learned how to deny valid claims. Most claimants don't realize that when their insurance company adjuster interviews them after a claim is submitted, they are trained to try to get information to deny a claim. All the questions are designed to get information they can compare to the original insurance application.

Any minor mistake in the initial insurance application is determined to be a material misrepresentation. The claims adjuster then states that they don't have insurance coverage because the material misrepresentation, in the original insurance application, would have stopped the company from issuing the policy. The insurance premium is refunded, and the claim is denied. Most claimants don't get lawyers, and the company avoids paying a claim.

The other phrase that Jamie was trained to use when denying a valid claim was pre-existing condition. When an injured claimant presents a claim, the adjuster is trained to search the medical records for anything remotely related to the present injury. Once this remote connection is found, the adjuster tells the claimant they can't pay because the injury was a pre-existing condition. If the claimant doesn't get a lawyer, the claim is never paid.

Because of Jamie's excellent record of successfully denying valid claims, her supervisors at Northern Trust promoted her after five years to the newly formed HMO division. On the surface, HMOs looked like a good idea. Insurance companies would approach doctors and offer to send all of their policyholders to cooperating doctors. In return, the doctors would agree to reduce their normal charge because of the increased volume. This would allow the insurance companies to reduce the premiums charged to the business owners, and everyone would prosper and be happy.

In the past, most health insurance companies operated on a "fee for service" type plan. Under this plan, doctors that the patient chose would examine the patient, order the treatment, and the insurance plan would pay for the majority of the cost.

Patients went to doctors who had good reputations and got good results. Doctors that helped patients get better were rewarded with referrals of new patients. Doctors decided which tests and treatments were reasonable and necessary.

From the viewpoint of the insurance company, they had to pay the medical bills because the doctor stated the treatment was reasonable and necessary. Modern tests and procedures became more expensive, and the insurance companies started complaining about the cost. They increased the premiums to policyholders. Insurance adjusters, with business training, started asserting that new treatments were not reasonable and necessary to save the companies money. But it was hard to find doctors who would contradict other doctors about treatment plans. Without a contradictory medical opinion, the insurance companies generally had to pay medical claims.

The insurance companies then created a health care crisis. A well-financed public relations campaign convinced state legislators to allow HMOs to combat the "health care crisis." Managed care was the new method. In reality, it allowed the insurance companies to profit even more.

It took a few years for the HMO plans to go into effect. However, because business owners were offered health insurance for their employees at a lower rate, the trend towards HMOs expanded at an exponential rate. The HMOs convinced young doctors to work with them, promising them a large number of patients if they would cut their normal charges. In turn, the older, more experienced doctors started losing patients because they weren't on the HMO list. They were then forced to reduce their charges to get on the HMO list.

Most policyholders and taxpayers couldn't care less that their doctors were making less money. However, the quality of care was diminished because doctors cut their overhead by firing office workers and staff. It was impossible to give the same level of care with less people taking care of more patients.

There were also hidden evils of HMOs that most people didn't realize. The insurance industry had discovered how to get doctors to disagree with other doctors. Insurance companies would hire doctors as consultants with six figure fees. These company doctors would then make up arbitrary rules, denying proper care that would save money for the company.

Participating doctors were doctors that were part of the HMO. Insurance companies had two powerful tools at their disposal to keep these doctors in line. The first tool was the bonus program where the doctors received their normal fees plus yearly bonuses. At the end of the year, doctors were given a bonus based on how profitable the HMO was. This was a major financial incentive for doctors not to order expensive tests for their patients.

The second tool of the HMO was more ominous. There was a clause in the contract between the doctor and the HMO that stated either side could terminate the contract with 30 days notice to either side. If the business managers of the HMO thought a doctor was ordering too many tests and spending too much money, they could terminate the contract with the doctor. This could be financially devastating to a doctor since the majority of his patients come from HMOs. In addition, the industry practice is to blackball a doctor that has been terminated from another HMO. Other HMOs won't hire him because he's labeled as a problem. The doctor is then forced to work for another doctor, or at a government hospital, at a greatly reduced rate of pay.

Over the years Jamie tired of denying valid claims. The company profited, and she received bonuses based on the percentage of claims she didn't pay. After 10 years with Northern Trust, she gave a 30-day notice that she was taking the paralegal job with Karen Senard's Law Office.

Before she started with Karen's office, Jamie married her long time boyfriend of four years, Tom. They boarded a plane to Miami, where they planned to honeymoon. The plane had a malfunctioning electrical system and crashed in the Everglades. Jamie was one of 12 survivors on the plane, but she was paralyzed from the waist down and restricted to a wheelchair. Tom died on impact.

Jamie filed a lawsuit against the airline for the wrongful death of Tom and her injuries. She didn't know that her boss at Northern Trust had gone to Notre Dame with the risk manager of the airline. During the litigation, the risk manager asked her former boss for any dirt on Jamie to reduce the value of the lawsuit. After a week of asking co-workers about Jamie, the dirt was exposed.

A year and a half before the marriage, Tom and Jamie had a fight. She went out with some co-workers, got drunk, and had a one-night fling with another adjuster. Tom and Jamie worked out their problems, and the fling was never mentioned. This information was relayed to the airline's lawyers.

The judge ordered mediation before trial. At mediation, the airline's attorneys told Jamie and her attorney that they were going to use this information to show that the marriage probably would not have lasted long, since Jamie cheated on Tom while they were engaged. Jamie was humiliated and couldn't believe her old company would be so vindictive. Based on Tom's earning capacity, the lawsuit was worth seven to eight million. Jamie settled for one million because she didn't want her fling brought out in open court for the whole world, including Tom's family, to see. Her disdain for insurance companies was complete.

Jamie had six months of physical rehabilitation after the crash, but the mental rehabilitation took longer. Before the accident, she was a long-distance runner and a golfer.

When she was treated for depression, her doctors suggested a hobby to keep her busy. Since Jamie had always been a computer whiz, she used her extra time to learn all about computer construction and computer security systems. One of her few joys in life was breaking into a company's computer system. Jamie's knowledge of computer systems was extremely beneficial to Karen's law practice. At the beginning of a new case, Karen secured a court order to allow her firm to search the doctor's and hospital's computer for past e-mails and memos concerning the subject matter of the litigation.

Most people don't realize that when an e-mail or memo is deleted, that it stays in the system's hard drive. Someone with detailed computer knowledge, such as Jamie, could search the hard drive and find all of the past e-mails and memos about the malpractice case. Over the years, Jamie had found some very embarrassing and harmful material in computers of doctors and hospitals. This powerful evidence led to a number of large settlements for Karen's law office. Since Karen was working on a 40% contingency fee, she prospered quite nicely. Jamie always received a large bonus upon settlement of any case resulting in a six-figure fee.

Jamie didn't belong to any church, however, she considered herself a spiritual person and wanted to help those that weren't as fortunate. She donated 15% of her income to the Legal Aid Society, which provides free legal services to poor people.

Jamie and Karen became friends and worked very well together. Jamie's intelligence and her hatred of insurance companies fit perfectly with Karen's views of negligent doctors and the insurance companies that protected them.

* * * * *

Karen yelled across the hall, "Jamie, come in here and look at this response from Dr. Elsworth on the Martin lawsuit. He has Fast Eddie as his defense lawyer, and he filed a third party lawsuit against LAMPCO."

Jamie McDaniel rolled her wheelchair into her boss's office and read the complaint while Karen got coffee for both of them.

"Fast Eddie has never defended a malpractice claim in his life. Why does Dr. Elsworth have him as a lawyer?" Jamie asked as she reread the response.

"I don't know, but I love how they're shifting the blame to the HMO. We can sit back and watch 'em fight. We might be one of the first lawsuits that attack an HMO successfully. They normally can hide behind legal defenses that shift blame to the doctor. However, by alleging criminal conduct, they're exempt from the normal protections. This is a very good legal theory—I didn't think Fast Eddie had it in him," Karen said happily.

Jamie shook her head. "I don't like it. It's very unusual to have the doctor blame an HMO because that means he loses all of their business. LAMPCO was in *The Wall Street Journal* last month as the most profitable insurance company with the highest growth expectations. Why would a young doctor take on an HMO and lose business?"

Karen didn't know the answer to the very good question, but she decided to call Fast Eddie and ask him. Like most lawyers, Fast Eddie and his staff worked on Saturday mornings. After he purposely left her holding for 10 minutes for the sport of it, Fast Eddie got on the phone.

"How ya doing Karen? Are you still filling up those silk blouses of yours? You always look like 15 pounds of potatoes pushed into a 10-pound bag."

"Eddie, I'd forgotten how you can't open your mouth without trying to insult someone. It's a unique talent. My breasts are doing just fine, thank you. Enough small talk. Why are you defending Dr. Elsworth? No insurance company would hire you."

"Miss Karen, you're correct. No insurance company would hire me, but Dr. Elsworth let his premium payments lapse to his malpractice carrier, so he has no malpractice insurance. We were considering filing bankruptcy, but we wanted to see if we could get you to go after LAMPCO instead. How about if we meet over drinks at happy hour, and I tell you about LAMPCO."

Karen was stunned as she realized the problems with her formerly very good case. But Karen didn't want to appear too anxious. "I don't know about drinks; I'm feeling a little under the weather. How about lunch next week?"

"That's fine, baby doll. Ya let me know when, so I can start dreaming about ya."

"Next Wednesday, noon at the Hilton. Oh, and Eddie, be careful what you ask for, you might get it."

Karen correctly guessed that Eddie used his sexism to try to get an upper hand when dealing with female attorneys. Eddie thought women attorneys divulged information when they were angry to try to show their superior knowledge. Karen was not like most women attorneys; she knew how to throw the sexism back to men in a way that made them want to please her.

Karen knew this case was going to be very difficult. If she won a big verdict against the defendant doctor, he would be judgment proof because he doesn't have malpractice coverage. She couldn't go after LAMPCO without Dr. Elsworth's testimony. However, it appeared that the doctor was ready to expose the corrupt dealings of LAMPCO. If a jury were allowed to see LAMPCO's claims practices, the jury verdict could be astronomical. In addition, the media coverage potential was very high. Karen loved the free advertising she got from favorable news reports. However, Karen conceded to herself that turning the case into money for her clients was going to be hard.

Chapter 6

Dr. Chadwick "Chad" J. Elsworth III had an impressive background. His parents were both schoolteachers and raised him in Nashville, Tennessee. Class work came very easily for him, as did sports. He was captain of the football and baseball teams his senior year in high school. He went to Vanderbilt on a baseball scholarship, where he concentrated on his studies. He had a part-time job as a gas station attendant on the midnight shift, which allowed him to study when there were no customers. However, he made time for baseball, booze, and women, in that order. He worked hard and played hard.

Chad's handsome face and his tall, athletic body always attracted females of assorted ages and races. He always had a girlfriend but never developed any long-term relationships. He took perverse pleasure in asking a girl for her phone number and then never calling her.

After Vanderbilt, he went to medical school at Emory in Atlanta. While in medical school, he worked as a bartender on weekends. He couldn't wait to graduate and get a real job, making up for years of sacrifice. He dreamed of new cars, boats, and expensive vacations. He continued to excel academically in medical school and graduated with honors.

While in his residency at Dunwoody General Hospital in Atlanta, Chad met his wife, Sarah Anne Ferguson. She was the daughter of the chief surgeon at Dunwoody General. She had just finished the relaxed six-year plan at the University of Georgia. She took great pride in tracing her ancestry back to an original family that settled in Savannah before the Revolutionary War. When she bragged to her sorority friends about it, she conveniently forgot to mention that her forefathers came to Georgia because they were freed from a debtor's prison in England.

Sarah was of average height, fair-skinned with dark green eyes. Her daily aerobics kept her full figure nicely toned. Her father allowed her unlimited use of his credit cards, so Sarah was always dressed in the latest fashion. Her curly brunette hair usually had a bow in it because she enjoyed the preppy look. During college, her official major was childhood development. Her unofficial major, and main joy in life, was the Phi Mu sorority. Her senior year she was elected president and that had been the highlight of her life since then.

While at Georgia, Sarah had only dated starters on the football team. They were fun, but unfortunately didn't produce any long-term prospects. After graduation she decided to get her career on the fast track before she married. Both

Cosmopolitan and *Mademoiselle* said that was best. After college, Sarah didn't fit in easily to the real world. Her first job ever was as a social worker in the inner city of Atlanta. She'd never been exposed to the problems of poverty. She interviewed families to find out if they were eligible for welfare, and she was scared when she had to go out in the field to interview applicants at their homes. It was much simpler when she read about it in her schoolbooks.

After two months of working in the real world, she was miserable. She had an hour commute in the morning and at least twice that in the afternoons because of road construction. She was late almost every day to her aerobics class, and her friends were starting to talk.

After starting her new job, she told her dad she no longer needed an allowance because she was determined to support herself. At the time she made that decision, she felt independent and grown up. However, her paycheck could barely pay for her expensive apartment and her car insurance. Sarah knew she could not keep putting her pedicures, manicures, facials, and shopping on her credit cards.

After two months of being a career woman, Sarah developed a very strong maternal instinct. Sarah wanted to get married, quit her job, and have children. She decided her future husband would support her and allow her to raise her children in an appropriate manner. She was fortunate enough to have the looks and intellect to accomplish her goal, not to mention the right last name.

Chad was introduced to Sarah at the Hospital's Christmas party. The physical attraction was magnified by the business advancement opportunities for Chad. However, he didn't realize Sarah had the same motivations. She was pregnant by June of the following year and correctly gambled that Chad would marry her. Although he wasn't ready for marriage, he felt since her dad was his boss, there was no other alternative.

After the honeymoon, Chad needed a vacation. Since he couldn't leave his pregnant wife and go out of town, he settled for an afternoon of golf with his buddy from medical school, Dr. Charles "Trip" Cleland III. Trip worked at Atlanta Memorial Hospital in the emergency room as a trauma surgeon. He was single and planning to stay that way.

After the first hole, Chad complained to Trip, "I had no idea what marriage would be like. She wants so much of my time."

"I told you that your life was going to change. She probably has you on a schedule today," Trip correctly guessed.

"We have dinner at 7:00 sharp, and I can't be late. It's so hard to relax anymore. I'm tired all the time and worried about the future. Before I met Sarah, I thought I made a good salary."

"You know what they say, 'Behind every successful man is a woman that made it necessary,'" Trip chided.

Trip grabbed two beers from the cooler, tossed one to Chad, and asked, "Seriously, what's bothering you?"

"I don't feel I have enough energy to do my rounds at the hospital, keep up with the medical journals, and make Sarah happy. God forbid when the twins come."

"Twins! You didn't tell me you are having twins. No wonder you're scared."

"God is getting back at me for all the women I treated badly. He's giving me twin girls."

The two friends finished the front nine holes and stopped for more cold beer at the snack bar. As they were heading to the back nine, Chad continued to complain about his lack of energy. Trip reached into his pocket and pulled out a pill bottle. He took a pill and gave one to Chad.

"Take this and you'll feel better. Trust me, I'm a doctor."

Chad examined the dark blue, nameless pill and asked, "What is it? I want to know what it is before I take it."

"It's your solution. Listen to your doctor and take it. I'll tell you when we finish the round."

Chad shot a 42 on the front nine. He normally shot in the upper 30s. After the pill his improved shots were longer and straighter. He made an eagle on a par five—his first ever. The energy he felt running through his veins was wonderful, and even though he missed his putt on the eighteenth hole, he shot a 32 on the back nine. It was his best score ever on nine holes. As a bonus, he still had excess energy, so he got a large bucket of balls and practiced on the range. Trip sat on the bench, savored his beer, and smiled at Chad.

"Just what the doctor ordered. Trip, tell me the secret—I need this pill!"

"Amphetamines. Speed. It works, but don't take it every day. Just when you need a boost."

Chapter 7

Chad was learning firsthand the power of the HMO over the doctor. In his first three years of practice, his net income went down five percent per year. If it weren't for his yearly bonuses from the HMOs, his income would have gone down 10 percent per year. Chad decided to cut his overhead by firing his billing director. He took computer lessons and did the billing himself. This was an additional 15-20 hours a week added to his normal 80-90 hours. There was one benefit—he had to spend less time at home with Sarah.

The three-year-old twins, Linda and Laurie, were a handful. Sarah had complained non-stop since Chad fired the babysitter. He reasoned if Sarah wasn't working, she could care for the children. Sarah complained that took time away from the Junior League and her aerobics class. She constantly reminded Chad that the twins had given her stretch marks, and she needed the time at the gym. One day when Chad suggested the cheesecake and ice cream might bear some responsibility, his twice-monthly sex allowance was suspended for a month. After his suspension, he no longer responded to Sarah's complaints.

Chad had been using speed since the golf outing with Trip. He'd gotten by with using it twice a week for the past three years. He needed the energy to keep up with the practice and reasoned he wasn't an addict because he didn't use it every day, or on holidays or vacations.

Chad felt constant financial pressure from his practice and from Sarah. Because of the constant friction, his sexual attraction toward her was diminishing daily. However, his sexual attraction toward the nurses at the hospital was growing daily. One nurse in particular caught his interest. Ginger Smith was definitely the cream of the crop.

Ginger Smith was a 24-year-old R.N. on a mission to marry a doctor. By the time of her sixteenth birthday, Ginger knew God had blessed her with a rare gift: her perfect body. She was one of the few girls that was not intimidated by a Barbie doll's figure during adolescence. She was the type of woman who made men restless and noncommittal with their girlfriends because they hoped, impossibly, to meet and marry a girl like her in the future.

Chad had his own grading system for beautiful women. The type "C" woman walks into a restaurant and every man notices. The type "B" woman walks into a restaurant and every man and woman notices. The women look the type "B" over and mentally note some minor flaw about her body. The type "A" woman walks into a restaurant and every man and woman notices. The women are extremely upset when they can't find any faults with her body.

Chad thought Ginger was a type "A" beautiful woman, with a brain. During high school and college, she became aware of the power she had over men. She had only to choose the man, and he would date her. No man had ever broken off a relationship with her. She enjoyed variety in men but was always in monogamous relationships, except for one regrettable night on her nineteenth birthday. She quizzed every man on sexual techniques, and none of them ever complained about the curious schoolgirl.

By the time she was in her junior year of college, Ginger had decided she wanted to become a nurse. There were two reasons. The first was that she found it rewarding to help people. The second, and most important reason, was that she wanted to marry a rich doctor and retire.

Ginger had come from a modest background. She wanted the country club lifestyle and to travel to all of the exotic places she read about in magazines. She didn't want to be a commoner, and it had always bothered her that her last name was "Smith." She wanted an uncommon name to go with her future uncommon plans.

Ginger's observation of the world was simple. Great athletes are paid a lot of money to play professional sports. Great intellects excel in school and are paid a lot of money for highly specialized careers. They are using the gifts that God gave them to succeed. God gave Ginger her body, which she was going to use to marry a rich doctor and enjoy a life of luxury.

Chad maintained his athletic body by daily five-mile runs. He was a handsome man and had all the expensive toys that a young doctor should have. He got a new Porsche every year and kept his cabin cruiser on nearby Lake Lanier, with the matching lime green Jet Skis stored on board. It didn't matter that he couldn't afford it, because he could have it now and pay for it later, somehow. He deserved it.

Ginger did her research on Chad, who had been checking her out on his rounds. The water cooler gossip was that he was unhappily married with two kids. She became extremely interested after she learned of his frequent Porsche purchases. She had dreamed of "his" and "her" Porsches since high school, so she decided to introduce herself to Chad. The first time she spotted him alone in the hospital cafeteria, she undid the top two buttons of her blouse as she approached.

"Hello, Dr. Elsworth. Do you mind if I join you?" She asked while pulling up a chair.

"Please, there's plenty of room," Chad replied as his face flushed.

"My name is Ginger, and I just started here at the hospital. I'm trying to meet everyone," Ginger said as she pulled her blonde hair away from her face.

Chad and Ginger exchanged their polite biographies.

While Chad talked to Ginger, he looked up and down her gorgeous body. When she caught him looking at her breasts, she smiled. He looked into her bright, blue eyes and blushed. Ginger could tell that Chad was under her spell and decided to use her research.

"I used to Jet Ski in college. I miss it so much. Do you know any place that rents them around here?"

Chad's mind raced as he debated being loyal to his frigid wife and mother of his children, or steal an afternoon with this young, beautiful, willing woman. The debate lasted less than two seconds.

He blurted out, "I have two Jet Skis on my cruiser. We ought to go this Saturday."

For the rest of the week, they met for lunch every day. They met for their first date that Saturday in the hospital parking lot. He picked her up in his red Porsche and they drove to Lake Lanier. It was a sunny spring day, and spring fever was running rampant.

Once they left the marina, Ginger went inside the cabin on the boat to change. Ginger went to a tanning salon twice a week. She came out with a black thong bikini and a smile. It was a vicious combination that made Chad dizzy. Chad drove his boat to an isolated area of the lake where he lowered the Jet Skis into the water. They rode around the lake jumping over boat wakes and racing each other. The warm day tired them out after two hours and headed back to the cruiser.

When they took a break from the Jet Skis, Chad made a pitcher of Bloody Marys. While they drank them, Chad gave her his prepared speech about why he had a bad marriage. Ginger listened intently to her competitor's flaws. After Chad finished talking about his bad marriage, Ginger stood up, stretched her arms up above her head, presenting her breasts for inspection and said, "I'm going to get a quick shower while you make some more drinks."

After Ginger showered, she walked out from the cabin nude and saw Chad drinking his Bloody Mary. He looked at her and felt his mouth go dry, and the veins in his neck pulsed like a strobe light.

Ginger smiled and said, "Bring that Bloody Mary into the cabin and I'll show you a new way to drink it!"

Ginger was pleased with herself after their first date. She got her man and his addiction to her was complete. It was a pleasant surprise to her that Chad was a good lover. After their first date, Chad and Ginger tried to arrange their schedules to meet during the lunch hour on weekdays and on Sunday nights. Ginger was using everything she had learned during her years of sexual research to please Chad. She decided Chad was going marry her and was looking for some sign of commitment after a month of hard work. She expected him to be divorced within the year, or she was going to switch to a different doctor.

After Sunday dinner at her apartment, Chad surprised her by asking, "What color Porsche do you want?"

Ginger squealed in excitement, "Red, cherry red. What other color is there?"

"I'll put $10,000 down and put it in your name, but I'll make the monthly payments. I'll get you the cherry red with the convertible top. How does that sound?" Chad asked innocently.

Chad was in over his head financially. Between his toys, his wife's shopping, and their standard of living, he was in a deficit, and that was before he got the expensive girlfriend. He was in a hole, but his ego told him he could work himself out of it. He decided to cut things from his budget that he could get by without. His life insurance was first, because the premiums were $18,000 a year. If he died, he didn't care what happened to Sarah. He did care about the twins, but his father-in-law had money and would take care of them, Chad reasoned. The next cut was his malpractice insurance because Chad listened to his ego. He knew he was a good doctor and thought he'd never make a mistake. The premium was $20,000 a year, and he knew this money could be spent in a better way.

Chad was thrilled and excited about life with Ginger, so he wanted to give her gifts to keep her happy. He knew she was a gold digger, but he didn't care. He enjoyed how she prospected. Ginger was taking Chad's remaining energy and time, so he increased his speed to daily doses. He knew it was bad for him, but he justified that it was just short term until he decided between Sarah and Ginger.

Chad's practice was becoming increasingly harder because of the HMO restrictions. Before he could order a medical test for patients, the HMO had to approve it. The HMO adjusters were telling him how to practice medicine. When he argued with them, they reminded him he had the option of not participating in the program. The adjusters took secret pleasure in putting doctors in their place. The adjusters reasoned that most of these expensive tests weren't worth the money. Sure, there would be a few patients harmed, but it was an acceptable risk.

LAMPCO was the worst HMO to deal with. It seemed to Chad that they denied all MRI tests. They suggested other tests that were less expensive. The other tests were helpful, but not as good as MRIs. Chad had spent the past year fighting with LAMPCO over their policy. They were a new company, but had gotten a large market share because of their low premiums. LAMPCO reminded Chad that they could find another doctor to refer patients to. Chad backed down because he knew he could never afford a reduction in his income.

Chapter 8

The acronym of LAMPCO stood for Leading Alliance of Medical Professionals Company. LAMPCO was founded by Theodore Marion and was one of the best performing stocks on the stock exchange. It was an HMO that specialized in cost-control medicine and affordable premiums for business-es of all sizes. These buzzwords, along with the company's unnatural profits, had many companies looking to buy out LAMPCO.

Theodore Marion, the CEO of LAMPCO, was born and raised in Hartford, Connecticut, to a privileged lifestyle. Theodore was tall, thin and had no tolerance for people with political views different from his conservative views. He got his undergraduate business degree from Harvard and his MBA from the University of Chicago. While Theodore was getting his MBA, he had a few friends that experienced unplanned pregnancies with their girlfriends. He decided he never wanted to worry about unplanned pregnancies, so he got a vasectomy. However, before the vasectomy he went to a sperm bank and opened up a savings account for him-self and made deposits. If he ever wanted to have children, he would make a withdrawal and have his wife artificially inseminated, at his discretion.

Theodore was married and divorced three times before he was forty, but he never told his wives about his vasectomy. He decided he was not ready for children, so he never gave any of his wives his prized, stored specimens. However, he did give his third wife herpes immediately before the divorce.

His first job after he graduated with his MBA was as corporate sales manager in the southeast region for Great States Insurance Company. He exceeded all of his sales quotas and was promoted to district manager of the southeast region. After his problematic promotion party, he hired Alvin "Al" Brognese as his personal assistant.

*   *   *   *   *

Alvin "Al" Brognese was the third of nine children from a second generation Italian family in Philadelphia. He was short and stocky with a receding hairline. His black eyebrows were growing together and overshadowed his small, intense eyes. His stare was intimidating because his dark brown eyes were nearly the same color of his pupils and they appeared to be reptilian.

Al was the first member of his family to go to college. He graduated in the middle of his class at Temple and took a sales job with Great States Insurance in the corporate sales division in Philadelphia. He did very well selling business and medical insurance to his family members that ran local trucking and shipping concerns.

Most of Al's family worked at blue-collar jobs, but a few of his cousins worked for the local Mafia, although they told people they worked in customer relations. The rest of Al's family took pride in having a direct connection to the Family. Whenever they said "Family" they would lower their voice and draw out the "a" in a manner that would make Marlon Brando proud.

After their weekly Sunday dinner, Al, his father, and three brothers would go to the front porch after dessert and discuss the local gossip while smoking Partagas robusto cigars. After the news was discussed, the male members of the Brognese family would then debate the perfect murder. It was a family tradition.

Al's father always liked an icicle in the ear because there was no entry or exit wound. The icicle would puncture the brain and melt, leaving no murder weapon. Since there was no murder weapon, there would be no fingerprints. One day Al asked his father where would he get the perfect-sized icicle when he was ready to commit a murder. Al's father muttered something about pulling it out of Al's ass.

Al's oldest brother, Dominic, liked the idea of burning the house down after he tied up the victim and cut their neck.

Dominic reasoned that the fire would destroy all of the evidence. It also penalized the remaining family members since they had nowhere to live.

Al's middle brother, Tony, liked to fake a robbery. He suggested using a .22 caliber pistol, since it was the most common weapon for street crime. The victim's wallet and watch would be taken. You would give some neighborhood kid $100 to tell the police that he saw some black guy running after he heard the shots.

Al's youngest brother, Danny, suggested breaking into the victim's home and putting arsenic on the victim's medicine. The victim would take the tainted pill and die. Many victims had heart attacks while the poison was killing them. If they didn't have a heart attack, an autopsy would show the poison, but the police normally look at family whenever a victim is poisoned.

Al's family always pressed him to choose his perfect murder, but he would never commit to one universal choice. His standard answer was that each situation was different, but you should always hire a professional and let them do the job. He would get annoyed with his family's weekly fantasy about murder because he knew that none of them had the resolve to kill a man.

After 10 years with Great States, Al got transferred to Atlanta to work with the southeastern division. He was fortunate enough to get some good referrals from his extended family in Atlanta, and continued to advance in the company. Al's supervisor in Atlanta was Theodore Marion. They had two very different backgrounds and personalities, but they did have a common religion. They both worshipped money. He competed with 20 other salesmen in his division, but his sales numbers were average for the area, and he debated about how to get Theodore's attention and advance in the company. The opportunity presented itself at Theodore's promotion party.

Theodore was surprised that he got promoted to district manager because he was competing against others with more seniority. When the announcement was made at four in the afternoon on a Friday, the temptation for a party was overwhelming. Great States' office was located in Marietta, a northern suburb of Atlanta. The rolling hills and distance from the problems of the inner city made Marietta a very attractive area for corporate headquarters. Theodore and his brown-nosing friends went to his favorite bar, Darryl's, and stayed until closing time.

Al realized that Theodore would need a ride home and had quit drinking early in the evening because he calculated it was an easy way to get on the good side of his boss. At closing time, Al was the only one left watching Theodore kissing his secretary, Jane Sesins. Everyone else had left when Jane sat on her boss's lap and gave him a long, wet kiss. When Al told Theodore he was going to drive him home, Theodore became angry and refused. Theodore insisted on driving Jane home in her car, so Al convinced Theodore that he should at least follow them to her apartment to make sure he was safe. Theodore and Jane were hanging onto each other as they giggled and stumbled to her car.

Al followed behind the weaving car, cutting through the early morning fog and barely staying on the curvy roads through the hills. Al could see Jane leaning across the seat, kissing Theodore on the neck. Luckily, there were no oncoming cars as Al watched Jane slide her head down, out of sight, and Theodore reposition himself in the seat. The speed of Jane's car increased as it raced through the dark country roads.

Theodore never saw the deer as he rounded the curve. Once the doe saw the headlights, she froze. Theodore only put on the brakes after he hit the deer. His car went into a slide and the front right tire hit the grass, and the brakes caught. Like many drunk drivers, Theodore overcorrected and the car went up on its right wheels for about three seconds as it continued its slide off the road. Gravity finally pulled it down as it slid off the pavement into a sloping field where the car traveled about 50 yards before it slammed into a large pine tree.

Al pulled his car off to the side of the road, jumped out, and got a flashlight from his trunk. He started to run down the hill but slipped on the dew-covered grass. He tumbled down the hill until his legs became entangled in a patch of Kudzu growing over and around the nearby pine trees. He pulled himself from the broken vines and felt the grainy sap all over his body.

Al stood up and felt the pain of a twisted left ankle. As he hobbled down the hill, he smelt the burnt rubber and leaking gas. The blue Chevy Cavalier was turned on the passenger's side, with the roof leaning against a broken tree. He climbed up the side and looked through the broken window. He saw Jane's head wedged under the bent steering wheel and the steering column. Her body was twisted back and stretched on the floorboard with her left leg twisting in the air. He looked at her blank, wide-open eyes and didn't bother checking her pulse because she was obviously dead. Al saw Theodore upside down in the back seat leaning against the right rear door. He looked pathetic with his gray pants and his purple silk boxers hanging around his ankles.

Theodore was rubbing his head and when he saw Al, he pleaded weakly, "Help. Help me."

Al said, "Give me your hand, and I'll pull you out."

Al pulled Theodore from the wreckage and helped him pull his pants back up. Al carefully led him up the hill to his black Lincoln town car and put his whimpering boss in the back seat while he surveyed the scene. The dead doe was on the side of the road and no other cars had been by the accident scene. Al had a bottle of Chivas Regal in his trunk leftover from the Christmas party. He grabbed the bottle and went back down to the crashed car. He could smell leaking gas, so he knew there wouldn't be a problem with the fire.

Al pushed the leaning car from the roof and caused it to settle back on its tires. One of the headlights was still shining and created eerie shadows on the Kudzu. He rearranged Jane's body in the car so she appeared to be driving. He pulled Theodore's jacket from the back of her car and made sure nothing fell from the pockets during the crash. He poured half of the Chivas Regal on Jane's hair and clothes. He pulled his handkerchief out and made a Molotov cocktail with the remaining booze. He walked about 10 feet from the car, lit the handkerchief and threw the bottle into the car. There was an immediate inferno in the car. Al made it back to his car before the explosion occurred. Theodore was crying and apologizing when he got back to the car.

Theodore said through his tears, "It's my fault, I should've seen the deer. It felt so good when she was doing it, I shut my eyes. What do I tell the police?"

Al slapped him and said firmly, "There'll be no police. Listen to me—Jane was drunk and when she was driving home, she ran off the road and killed herself. She died instantly from a broken neck and then burned in the resulting fire. Got it? I drove you to my house from the party and you slept on my couch. You don't know anything about this crash. Got it?"

Theodore mumbled some more about the accident being his fault and started to cry. Al hit his boss with a strong right cross and knocked him out. Al pulled him from the back seat and positioned him in the front passenger seat, strapping the seatbelt around him. Al drove Theodore away from the accident scene, very pleased with himself, thinking the Kennedys weren't the only family that can fix an accident.

Chapter 9

After 10 years with Great States Insurance Company, Theodore and Al saw a great opportunity for profit in the HMO business. They decided to start their own company, so they recruited investors and founded LAMPCO. Theodore and Al agreed to waive a salary for the first two years if they were each given 10,000 shares of stock in LAMPCO. The investors were impressed with the confidence of Theodore and Al, and readily agreed to the offer.

LAMPCO hired aggressive salesmen and gave them a lucrative product to sell. LAMPCO's premiums were 20% lower than other HMO companies. Sales increased rapidly, and every month a new record was broken. Doctors were lining up to be a participating doctor with LAMPCO and get more patients. Theodore and Al had spent a number of years in the insurance business, and they knew they had a gravy train to wealth if they could deny valid claims. However, they needed a doctor that was willing to lie and claim some medical procedures were not reasonable and necessary.

They decided to hire the best doctor that was for sale. Dr. Bennete was hired away from a competitor HMO. At 62,

Dr. Bennete had a substantial amount of money in the bank, but he wanted more. LAMPCO hired him for $300,000 a year for medical consultation. Dr. Bennete's job was to review requests for service and issue his medical opinion on whether the tests were reasonable and necessary for treatment of a patient. He would've been a very busy man if he had actually looked at each patient's request for treatment. But he never looked at any cases; he just signed his name on any report denying medical treatment that the business managers for LAMPCO deemed were not reasonable and necessary.

Doctors that participated in LAMPCO's HMO plan were required to carry a 10 million-dollar malpractice policy. If a patient were injured or died because of malpractice caused by LAMPCO not approving a test, the doctor's insurance plan would cover the loss. No doctor would blame LAMPCO because they wouldn't approve a test. If that happened, the doctor would be dropped as a participating doctor from LAMPCO and be blackballed from other HMOs. His practice and income would dry up. In addition, all of the states had laws prohibiting patients from suing their HMOs for denial of medical treatment. Different consumer groups lobbied the state legislatures for changes, but the insurance lobby made generous donations to the politicians to make sure no reforms were passed.

LAMPCO had the perfect scheme for short-term profit.

Their own doctor had given them a medical opinion, so they could show this report to any government regulator that might question the claim practices at LAMPCO. If a patient were injured or died because LAMPCO wouldn't approve a test, they would have to sue the doctor for malpractice. If any participating doctor were sued for malpractice, his insurance company would have to pay the claim. Theodore and Al decided to increase LAMPCO's profits by denying all MRI tests that weren't ordered by an emergency room doctor. Other tests could be ordered that were less expensive than MRI's. This plan was very profitable for LAMPCO. Businesses were trying to keep their health plan expenses down to increase their profits. Since LAMPCO had the cheapest premiums, they were getting the majority of the new business.

When LAMPCO's stock was initially offered, it sold for a dollar a share. Because of the large profits and increased number of policyholders, LAMPCO was now selling for $140 a share. It was rumored on Wall Street that other insurance companies wanted to buy LAMPCO because of their huge profits. Experienced stockbrokers thought that a larger insurance company would eventually buy out LAMPCO and estimated the buyout price to be in the $200 per share range.

Chapter 10

"Al Brognese, please come to the front desk. Al Brognese, please come to the front desk. You have a phone call," the hurried receptionist announced through the old speakers at the health club.

Al was not happy. He'd spent the last hour trying to get away from the office to get his workout in. If it was his wife, it'd better be an emergency. If it was his secretary, he'd fire her.

"This is Al. What is it?"

Theodore spoke rapidly in a nervous voice, "Al, get dressed and come to the office. We just got served with a lawsuit that could affect the buyout negotiations."

"We get sued all the time. What's the big deal?" Al asked angrily.

"Your family will not like this lawsuit, Al. It could affect their investment and ours. A lot. I can't talk about it over the phone. I called our lawyers, and they'll be here within the hour to meet with us and the management team," Theodore reported solemnly.

Al recognized the tone in Theodore's voice. He hadn't

heard that tone since the morning after Theodore's promotion party. He hung up and hurried to the showers with his mind racing over the possibilities. Lawsuits were never a good thing, but they were manageable. Something was very wrong because Theodore rarely brought up Al's family.

After Theodore and Al had quit Great States and founded LAMPCO, Al had told his extended family about the investment opportunities at LAMPCO. Al's family had invested one million dollars of pension money in LAMPCO's stock when it was selling for 12 dollars a share. It was now selling at 140 dollars a share. Al's family investment of one million was now worth almost 12 million.

Al and Theodore also had their 10,000 shares of stock that was now worth 1.4 million each.

When the company formed, LAMPCO had retained one of the oldest law firms in Atlanta, Prince and Wilson, to prepare the incorporation and stock sale certificates. Prince and Wilson had 85 lawyers in the firm and had grown rich over the past 75 years, defending insurance companies and railroads throughout the south. Don Welch, a senior partner, had represented LAMPCO since they were founded. He'd noticed how profitable LAMPCO had become and convinced his partners to invest one million dollars of their profit-and-share fund in LAMPCO. Prince and Wilson had bought their shares at 20 dollars per share, and their investment had grown to seven million dollars.

As Al was driving back to LAMPCO, he did the math in his head. The total dollars between him, Theodore, his family, and the law firm was 21.8 million. Any problem that could affect this money was unacceptable. Al always prided himself on staying calm in a crisis. For a moment, he felt panic start to enter his body, and his vision blurred as he became dizzy. Al quickly pulled off the road into a mall parking lot, where he stopped the car, turned off the radio, and shut his eyes. He concentrated on getting back in control and clearing his mind. After two minutes of deep breathing, he opened his eyes. His control was back, and he was ready to tackle this new problem. He had fixed problems before and he would fix this problem. Al calmly pulled his black Mercedes back into traffic and obeyed the speed limit as he drove to his office in downtown Atlanta. He was secure in his self-confidence and his past success.

*   *   *   *   *

Al entered the main conference room on the eighth floor of the administration building at LAMPCO. The large windowless room had a 20-foot oval mahogany table in the center. There were 12 men sitting in the burgundy, overstuffed, high-back chairs looking at Al. Before anyone could speak, Al quickly looked around the room to assess the body language. He felt the panic in his throat briefly and then forced it from his mind.

Don Welsh yelled across the room with the bravado expected of a seasoned trial attorney, "Al, this fucking doctor has claimed in a lawsuit that LAMPCO is systematically denying MRI's that are medically necessary, and it's a criminal scheme to defraud. I can't wait to take his depo. I'll make the son-of-a-bitch wish he was never born!"

Don was a tall, confident litigator. He had played forward for the North Carolina Tar heels in the late 1970s, but in his senior season he'd blown out his knee and ruined his chance for a pro basketball career. He still used his competitive fires from basketball in his law practice. His partners loved his abrasive tactics, but his opponents hated to deal with his "take no prisoners" approach to practicing law.

Al looked across the table at Theodore, his past and present partner in crime. He saw a pale, worried face looking to him for guidance. Theodore said nothing, and the rest of the management team looked to Al for a response. Al looked at Don, and the silence became deafening. Al took a deep breath and processed the situation quickly.

Al yelled to his management team, "Enough of this. This is nothing but a fucking greedy lawyer trying to extort money from us. Don't worry people, our lawyer will eat him up! Everyone go back to work; we'll take care of this. However, I need to warn everyone about keeping this quiet. Everyone here owns stock and will benefit tremendously if we're bought out. Don't leak news of this lawsuit to anyone. It could hurt the company, your family, and . . . my family."

Everyone gave a few nervous glances and most people forced a smile as the management team left. Al walked over to the heavy doors, shut them quietly, and turned around to look at Theodore and Don sitting uncomfortably at the table. Don could sense there was uneasiness in the silent room, so he finally broke the ice.

"What's the deal, guys? Why does this doctor have such a crazy idea? Do you know who his lawyer is? It's Fast Eddie. He's a fucking media hound! Do you know what a lawsuit like this can do to our stock prices if it's reported?"

Theodore finally spoke in a quivering voice, "How much money does your family have invested, Al?"

Al finally exploded, "Too much. This lawsuit, this doctor, this Fast Eddie lawyer, have got to be fixed! If my family loses 12 million dollars, all three of us will be breathing dirt!"

Don Welch protested in his best righteous indignation voice, "Now, wait a minute, I'm just a lawyer advising my clients. Why would your family come after me? That's not fair!"

Al yelled at his attorney as he glared defiantly at him, "Counselor, your big words and fancy arguments won't stop a bullet. If my family thinks you're responsible for losing their money, they'll gladly kill you. And you know what?

Before they kill me, I'm gonna to tell them this was all your idea, and you said we could get away with it."

Don Welch was not aware of the claims practices at LAMPCO. However, Al knew Don would work harder for LAMPCO if his life was at stake. He also knew that Don couldn't withdraw as attorney because of the investment his firm had in LAMPCO.

Al stoked his chin for a moment before he spoke in a quieter tone. "Counselor, I don't want to threaten you. But I can't control what my family might do. My family has blamed attorneys in other failed business ventures, and it was not pretty. I just think it's fair that I warn you of the consequences of losing this case."

For the first time in Don Welch's adult life, he was speechless. He couldn't believe that this short, fat, Italian man had just threatened his life. Don stared into Al's dark eyes and realized Al was serious about him dying if he lost the case. He thought of his wife and three teenage boys. He felt the growing pangs, deep in his bowels, warning of an imminent explosion, so he ran to the bathroom.

Fifteen minutes elapsed before Don returned to the conference room. During this time, Theodore's face was pale, and he said nothing. Al realized Theodore was going to be worthless during this crisis. Al sat in angry silence, disgusted by Theodore's cowardly reaction. Al pulled out a Partagas robusto cigar from his suit jacket and lit up as he contemplated the situation. He thought of Don looking down at him when he made the threat. Don was a tall, cocky lawyer that looked down at Al, literally and figuratively. Al had tired over the years of people looking down at him because he was short. Tall people seemed to question his resolve, and someone once told him that he had the Napoleon complex. Al quipped that a tall psychologist, to justify his inadequacies, invented the Napoleon complex.

When Don returned from the bathroom, he walked purposefully into the quiet room and glanced tentatively at Al and Theodore before he sat down quietly at the conference table. He thought of his ethics class in law school and how his professor had warned of the dangers of investing with a client. He silently cursed himself for not listening more closely.

Don looked at Al and said firmly, "I agree that this case must be won. I assure you I'll do everything within my power to win."

"I'm glad we understand each other." Al blew cigar smoke menacingly towards Don and stared at him for a few seconds before continued. "Understanding is a very important thing."

Don nodded and stammered, "I'll be at the library tonight searching every database for some type of case that will help us."

Al blew more smoke toward Don and smiled. "I don't

think you'll find the solution to our problem in any of your law books, but I might be wrong. You'll let me know tomorrow at breakfast, right?"

At this point, Don didn't care about ethics. He just wanted to live to see his three sons graduate from college. Don shifted in his seat and replied hesitantly, "Sure, breakfast. Where do you want to meet?"

Al had found a kindred spirit. He smiled and said, "The Cracker Barrel just up the road at I-85. See you at nine. Study hard counselor; we need to fix this problem."

Chapter 11

"I'm sorry, sir, that card has been declined also," the saleslady at Tiffany's jewelry store informed Chad.

"That's ridiculous; let me call the credit card company. May I use your phone?" Chad asked.

Chad had taken Ginger to Tiffany's at the Perimeter Mall over their lunch break. She'd been distant since he told her about the malpractice lawsuit and his lack of insurance. It was her twenty-fifth birthday, and he was going to buy her an emerald and diamond tennis bracelet. Ginger was thinking that maybe she'd been too hard on Chad, when the saleslady told them the first credit card was declined. When the second credit card was declined, she was furious.

Chad yelled angrily to the customer service representative over the phone. "What do you mean I've used up my credit? When was the last charge?"

"This morning at nine, Sarah Elsworth made a cash advance of $8,409.23. There is zero remaining available on your credit line," the customer service representative reported in a smug voice.

Chad hung up the phone, and he dialed the first credit

card's customer service line as fast as possible. He ignored the questions from Ginger and the stare from the saleslady. When the customer service representative answered the phone, Chad demanded to know the last charge on his account.

"The last charge on your account was this morning at 9:10 a.m. by Sarah Elsworth. She made a cash advance of $12,032.04. There is zero remaining on your credit line," reported the customer service representative.

Chad hung up the phone. He lied when he told the clerk he would come back later and pay in cash. He went outside with Ginger who stared straight ahead and said nothing as they walked to his car. She wondered if Chad could keep making payments on her Porsche if his credit cards were maxed out. She promptly shifted her thoughts to other doctors on the hospital staff that were available with better credit card limits.

Chad decided to partially lie to Ginger, "My wife has canceled our credit cards. I've got to find out what's going on."

Ginger said nothing as they drove back to the hospital in his Porsche. Chad dropped her off at the hospital and drove furiously to the bank. After an hour of calls and a meeting with the branch manager, he learned that between 9:00 a.m. and 10:30 a.m. his wife had managed to get $85,022.13 in cash advances on seven of their joint credit cards. She also closed their checking and savings accounts and got a cashier's check for the balance of $3,238.34. The bank manager said he was sorry, but there was nothing he could do.

Chad stumbled out of the bank in a daze. What was Sarah going to do with the money? Where did she put the money?

Chad drove back to his office. It was the lunch hour when he entered his office, and noticed a sheriff's deputy sitting in his empty waiting room. The deputy looked familiar.

The sheriff's deputy stood up. "Dr. Elsworth, I have divorce papers for you. I'm sorry, I know this has been a bad month for you."

The same deputy that had served the malpractice suit was now giving him notice of divorce papers filed that morning by his wife. Chad took the papers and said nothing as he sat down in his waiting room. The deputy left the office, secure in the knowledge that he'd have the best story to tell at happy hour with his buddies.

Chad sat in his empty waiting room because he didn't have the energy to move. His head started to pound as he read the divorce petition. She wanted half the assets, child support, permanent alimony, and she'd hired the most expensive and nastiest divorce attorney in Atlanta. Chad remembered one of the other doctors talking about having to pay his ex-wife's attorney bill from the divorce. Chad couldn't fathom how it was fair that he had to pay an attorney to take his money and children away from him. Chad felt his world slipping through his hands, so he closed his eyes and let his mind race. He was concentrating on how to hide his remaining money from his office account and drifted into a sleep with vivid, loud dreams that all ended with him driving a Yugo and living in a cheap apartment.

When his office staff started coming back from lunch, they were shocked to see their boss slumped back in a chair, his face white, eyes shut, and unresponsive to their greetings. When Chad finally awoke, he opened his eyes and saw his staff looking at him as if he were laying in a coffin at a viewing. When he came back to his senses, he excused himself and went back to his office.

He called his office manager into his office and told her to cancel his afternoon appointments. As Chad sat in his office, he thought about all the money his wife had taken and checked his wallet to find only a twenty. He quickly wrote a check from his office account for a thousand dollars. Fortunately, Sarah was not registered as a signatory on that account or his American Express business card. Chad drove to a different branch of his bank to cash his check to avoid embarrassment. After he cashed his check, he decided to go to his house to see what Sarah had done with the furniture and his clothes. As he drove home, he kept asking himself if Ginger had been worth it. He thought of the new experiences she had introduced him to and momentarily forgot his problems.

As Chad drove into his brick driveway, he saw a large U-haul truck backed up to his house. The two-story house was based on Tudor architecture, but the three-car attached garage didn't fit the Tudor theme, and Sarah's mother constantly reminded him of the one minor flaw in an otherwise perfect house. He parked his Porsche and walked around the truck to the front door of his house. He tried to open the door, but it was locked and his keys wouldn't open it. He walked to the garage door and saw the message taped to the door.

Chad,

My divorce lawyer told me to change the locks. All of your clothes and other shit is packed in the U-Haul. The keys are on the seat. I rented it for two days so you can decide where you are going to live. You sure as hell are not going to live in __my__ house!

I hope your girlfriend was worth it. I am going to take you for everything, you asshole!

Sarah

Chad felt the rage rise from his stomach, to his chest, and

then to his throat. The rage stuck in his throat and wouldn't allow him to form any words. The yell that came from his mouth was the sound of a tortured and cornered animal. He picked up a nearby potted plant and ran toward the kitchen window. He stopped a few feet short of the window and threw the potted plant at the window, shattering it instantly. He reached through the broken glass and opened the window, crawling into his house and standing up in the kitchen.

Sarah was upstairs and had seen Chad drive into the driveway. Her divorce lawyer told her to call the police when he arrived and say he was threatening her. As soon as she heard the crash, she called 911 and told the police her ex-husband was attacking her and she thought he was going to kill her. Sarah stayed locked in her bedroom until the police arrived. The police crashed through the front door and they found Chad sitting in his favorite leather recliner, drinking a beer, watching synchronized swimming on ESPN. Chad was bleeding from his arms as he sat in amazement watching the police point their guns at him in his family room.

Sarah came down and told the police he'd threatened to kill her. Chad tried to protest his innocence, but the police looked at the broken glass, his bleeding arm, and saw Chad turning red with anger. They arrested him for domestic violence and took him to jail. Chad was humiliated as he was handcuffed and put into the back of the squad car as his nosy neighbors watched. At the county jail he had his mug shot taken along with his fingerprints. He called Fast Eddie, who had Chad bonded out by six that night. The condition of his bond was that he stay away from his wife and their house. Chad called Trip from Fast Eddie's car phone and told him the events of the day. Trip told him to have Fast Eddie drop him off at his house for the night.

Trip met his friend at the door with a beer and a smile. "So, how was the jail, big guy?"

"It was fuckin' great, Mr. Smartass. Can you believe she's done this to me?"

"Yeah, I can believe it, and you can thank O.J. Simpson for it. Anytime a woman tells the police her husband has threatened her, you're going to jail. If you didn't want to kill her before you were arrested, you will after they take you to jail."

Chad shook his head in disbelief. "I didn't threaten her. I just wanted to watch T.V. in my house and drink a beer. Why can she lock me out of my house?"

"The woman always wins in divorce court, Chad. Accept it. You can't go back to the house, or see her, or you violate the terms of your bond. The cops will throw you back in jail and the judge won't set a bond. You will stay in jail until your trial date."

Chad chugged his beer and handed the empty bottle to Trip. "Give me a Dewar's—this beer isn't doing the job. I can't believe this is happening to me."

The two friends drank their Scotch in silence as they relaxed on the leather couch and watched ESPN. Watching ESPN reminded Chad of his single days when he had no responsibility other than work. They sat in front of the TV and enjoyed the high from the Scotch as they mindlessly watched Australian Rules football.

After they relaxed in silence and consumed three large glasses of Scotch, Trip spoke up, "You need a vacation."

Chad thought about it. Two lawsuits had been filed against him. His reputation as a doctor and his financial future were at stake. On the other hand, he certainly was in no frame of mind to work because he couldn't concentrate on anything. He definitely needed to get away from Sarah, because he was having problems controlling his anger. A week's vacation was a good idea. He was so far in debt, a little more didn't matter.

Chad said, "You're right. Where do you want to go?"

"Let's go to tarpon fishing down in Boca Grande where the fish are the size of a man. After fighting tarpon all day, you're so tired you can't move. Then back at the dock there are plenty of women and booze! What more could a man want?"

Chad thought for a second. Trip was born and raised in Boca Grande and always bragged about the natural beauty and good fishing. He was sick of Atlanta and his problems.

"Sounds great. Take care of the reservations. I don't

wanna think for the next week."

Chapter 12

Boca Grande is a small beach town on the Southwest coast of Florida located in Lee County. Ft. Myers, the county seat and largest city in Lee County, has a unique history because it was a Union fort during the Civil War. The Confederacy mostly ignored South Florida during the Civil War. The Union Soldiers operated Fort Myers, located on the Caloosahatchee River, to help facilitate cattle trade to the northern states to feed the soldiers.

When Florida became a state, Fort Myers was part of Monroe County, which covered most of South Florida. Because of local disputes, Ft. Myers successfully petitioned the Legislature in 1887 to make the Ft. Myers area into a new county. The proud southerners in Ft. Myers tried to atone for their town's dubious history as a Union Fort by naming the new county after the Confederate General, Robert E. Lee.

The barrier islands of Sanibel, Captiva, Upper Captiva, Cayo Costa, and Gasparilla protect Lee County from Gulf storms. Boca Grande is located on the southern tip of Gasparilla Island. On an incoming tide, the translucent, bluish-green waters of the Gulf of Mexico rush by the tip of Boca Grande into Charlotte Harbor. The mangrove lined rivers and creeks located east of the harbor empty their dark, tannin-stained waters into the harbor. On an outgoing tide, these dark waters mix with the gulf's water in the harbor to produce darker, hazy blue water. The baitfish and crabs of Charlotte Harbor swim with this outgoing tide to produce a perfect fishing spot at Boca Grande because the water is forced into a narrow funnel of water between Boca Grande and Cayo Costa. The roaring tide has produced a deep passage between the Harbor and the Gulf, called Boca Grande Pass.

Tarpon are large fish, silver in color, with a huge up-turned mouth. During May, June, and early July of each year, thousands of tarpon gather in Boca Grande Pass to feed before they begin their long swim to the continental shelf for their breeding duties. Their tough flesh is primarily muscle that allows a six-foot fish to jump 10 feet into the air when hooked. Tarpon are not good to eat, but their fighting style has earned them the nickname of the Silver King. Fishermen come from around the world to catch them in the early summer every year.

* * * * *

"Wake up! Wake up! The alarm went off 15 minutes ago," Trip barked as he shook Chad by the shoulders. "I'm already showered and dressed. The fishing guide is picking us up in 30 minutes. I'm going to the dining room and order us breakfast. At Cabbage Key you have two choices—eggs and bacon, or pancakes and bacon."

"Surprise me. I told you I don't wanna think this week," Chad growled as he stretched.

Chad awoke from his first deep sleep in months. He had to think for a minute where he was and what day it was. It was Tuesday morning, and they'd flown from Atlanta into the Ft. Myers airport the day before. Trip had rented a car at the airport and given the guided tour. Chad had been amazed at how the scenery had changed in the 45-minute ride to Pineland Marina.

The airport was in the middle of urban sprawl that decorated either side of Interstate 75. They took Daniels Parkway, a six-lane highway, from the airport to U.S. 41. Heading north on U.S. 41 carried them by an endless stream of strip malls into downtown Ft. Myers and across the wide Caloosahatchee River, which was a beautiful sight as they drove across it, and into North Fort Myers.

North Fort Myers seemed to be a magnet for every fast food restaurant and chain hotel in the nation. After a procession of slow red lights, they turned west onto Pine Island Road. The development gave way to wide open fields scattered with pine trees and real estate signs. After a few miles of visual freedom, they passed into Cape Coral. Cape Coral had its own strip malls scattered among the sporadic houses that were on the flat, treeless expanses of open fields. After they left the barren lands of Cape Coral, they entered Matlacha.

Matlacha is an old fishing village on a small island, situated among canals and bays that empty into the Matlacha River, which empties into Charlotte Harbor. As they passed over the three small bridges in Matlacha, Chad noticed the old shrimp boats and crab boats docked at ancient docks that looked like they would tip over from a good storm.

The speed limit slowed to 25 mph in Matlacha and they had to watch for old trucks pulling out in front of them, loaded down with the catches of the day. Deeply tanned bicyclists traveled with the traffic. Dogs patiently waited for a break in the traffic to cross the only paved street on the island community.

The small shops and restaurants in Matlacha were built up close to the road. Customers could only back out of the parking lots when there was a break in the traffic. The trucks, bicyclists, and dogs patiently cooperated on the common road. Chad wondered if Atlanta had ever been that small.

After leaving Matlacha, they continued down the only road onto Pine Island, a long, narrow island between the mainland and the barrier islands of Upper Captiva and Cayo Costa. Between the barrier islands and Pine Island were the smaller resort islands of Useppa and Cabbage Key. The marinas on Pine Island were embarkation points for these barrier and resort islands, which were accessible only by boat. Boats ferried all food and supplies onto the islands and all the garbage off the islands.

Chad and Trip traveled to the northern portion of Pine Island and turned left off the main highway onto a winding road. The sign had read, "Pineland Marina 3 miles." On the left side was *Blind Hog Groves*, which produced a very unique harvest of mango, guava, and other exotic fruits. On the right side, orange trees lined the road. The orange groves were separated by old wooden homes of original families on the island.

The groves gave way to mangrove trees as they got closer to the salt water. There was a break in the mangroves, and a U.S. Post Office appeared on the right. The building was about 15 feet square with three parking spaces. They could smell the salt water before they saw it. The curving road opened up onto a stunning view of Pine Island Sound. On the left side of the road, the water and oyster bars came up to within 10 feet of the road. Two bald eagles were diving into the water, their talons extended. They dove into the water simultaneously and both emerged carrying a trout.

On the right side, massive mounds of earth appeared on the flat land, some as high as 30 feet. Trip explained that these were ancient Indian mounds from the extinct Caloosa tribe. The mounds were made of shells that had been piled up generation after generation. The road continued to curve along the water, and a few houses appeared on the right and Tarpon Lodge on the left. A sign on the left showed they had arrived at Pineland Marina. They drove down the shell and sand road to the docks where they unloaded their luggage and waited for the water taxi. Four times a day, a large pontoon boat picked up passengers and ferried them to and from the resort islands.

They caught the last water taxi of the day at 6:00 p.m. As the boat glided over the calm water, a family of dolphins started following the boat. They got behind the boat and rode the wake like surfers on a beach, jumping out of the water and leaping over their competing family members. This performance lasted for about five minutes and thoroughly entertained the tourists. Chad totally forgot his own troubles, watching these happy creatures in the warm afternoon sun with the wind blowing through his hair.

After a 10-minute ride, the water taxi slowed as it entered the channel to Cabbage Key.

The island of Cabbage Key is about one half mile wide with the northern side developed and the remainder left in its natural state. It's a small, rustic resort with a main wooden building that has a restaurant and bar with seven hotel rooms for rent. For large parties, there are six cottages with their own docks for rent. The marina has the capacity for approximately 20 yachts. Other yachts and houseboats anchor in the adjacent basin when it's crowded. Smaller boats, bringing people for lunch or dinner at the restaurant, pull up on the sandy beach if the docks are filled. The main building is built on an Indian shell mound 38 feet high, making it the highest spot in Lee County. There are no swimming pools, tennis courts, televisions or phones in the rooms. The main attractions of Cabbage Key are fishing and relaxed time away from the mainland. It's rumored that Jimmy Buffet was so impressed with Cabbage Key that he wrote the song "Cheeseburger in Paradise" about his stay there.

Chad and Trip hauled their gear from the water taxi and walked up the Indian shell mound to the main lodge. After they unpacked, the cocktails flowed freely in the bar while the guitar player played everyone's favorite songs. There were the young and old in the lounge enjoying the music, as Chad finally relaxed. Atlanta and all of his problems seemed very far away. They ate a late dinner of surf and turf. Chad left Trip talking to a young lady and went back to their room suddenly exhausted by his problems and the journey. He laid down on the bed and fell asleep without taking off his clothes.

The smell of coffee drifted down to Chad's room and brought him back to the present. He quickly showered and dressed. The prospect of fishing excited him like a kid on Christmas morning. He hadn't felt that feeling in many years. He walked down the hall to his waiting breakfast of eggs and bacon. The waitress brought him a hot cup of coffee as he devoured his breakfast. It seemed his appetite had increased since he'd been around the salt water.

Chad and Trip were eating in the dining room next to the screened window. The morning breeze was far more comfortable than air conditioning. They had a commanding view of the marina as they ate breakfast. The early morning sun created long shadows on the island as the docks bustled with activity, people preparing their boats for a day of fishing.

Trip excitedly reported, "Look, there's our boat coming down the channel. It's a 42-foot Hatteras named *Two Tongues*. It's the best boat I've ever fished on. Captain Sandy Harper is a local guide, and he knows the best spots. Hurry up and finish—it's time to catch a tarpon."

Chad asked, "What's the biggest tarpon you ever caught?"

Trip proudly pointed to the six foot mounted tarpon hanging from the dining room's wall and said, "I boated one about a foot bigger than that one on the wall. We released it, but Sandy estimated it to be 270 pounds."

Chad finished his breakfast and they sprinted down to the docks for a day of pursuing the Silver King.

Chapter 13

Captain Ron "Sandy" Harper was a third generation Boca Grande fishing guide.

Sandy was 6'2" and lean with muscles hardened by his many years of living the hard life of a fishing guide. Outside of the four years playing wide receiver at Florida State, he'd lived in Boca Grande all of his 42 years.

His maternal grandmother was a Seminole Indian. He inherited her skin coloring that magnified his deep tan from living outdoors. His paternal grandfather was Swedish, and he inherited his ice-blue eyes and blond hair. The salt water and sun had bleached his long blond hair even lighter. Sandy's inherited genes and physical, outdoor lifestyle had blended perfectly to produce a confidant, charming ladies' man.

Sandy had never married, because of his strong independent streak and the stories of his charters. Of all his male charters, the majority complained about their marriage or how much their divorces had cost them. Of all his female charters, all but a few had hit on him. Especially the married, neglected, bored ones. These women had a strong, hidden libido that produced some of his most memorable affairs. He often wondered if their husbands knew what they were missing, while they were playing golf with their buddies and complaining about their marriages.

Sandy's longtime First Mate was Miguel Torres. Miguel was an illegal Mexican immigrant who had worked for Sandy for eight years. He helped prepare the riggings and assisted the angler while fishing. It was hard work but paid better than working at the farms, and he had a wife and four children to support. At the end of the day, he cleaned the fishing boat until it shined. Miguel also assisted the marina mechanic with his weekly tune-ups of the engines. The *Two Tongues* was the finest boat in the Boca Grande fishing fleet.

Sandy maneuvered *Two Tongues* next to the dock at Cabbage Key. Terry, the dock master, watched with admiration as the boat slowed and drifted within inches of the worn pilings without touching them. Terry took the lines from Miguel and secured them to dock's pilings.

"Good morning, Terry. How's that pretty wife of yours?" Sandy asked as Miguel began rigging the fishing poles.

"She's doin' great. When are ya going to settle down and get married, Sandy?"

"I'm not the marrying type. Me getting married is like tryin' to make a lap dog out of a Great Dane."

"Here comes your charter," Terry said as he walked

down the dock towards the next approaching boat.

Sandy looked down the dock and raised his voice. "Howdy, Trip! How's it going?"

Trip gave the thumbs up sign "It couldn't be any better. Sandy, this is my friend from Atlanta, Dr. Chad Elsworth."

"How's it going, doc?"

Chad replied, "I'm glad to be here. I've never been salt water fishing before."

Miguel untied the ropes as Trip and Chad got into the boat. Sandy eased down the channel, past the tip of Cabbage Key toward the Intercoastal Channel. Chad was intrigued by the pelicans diving on the schools of baitfish on the flats next to the channel. The wind was out of the south and produced a small chop on the water. Once away from the marina at Cabbage Key, Sandy powered his boat up on plane at 35 mph and headed north. The *Two Tongues* slicing through the water produced a four-foot wake behind the boat. The smaller boats in the channel had to slow as they crossed the wake. The owners of the smaller boats looked at the *Two Tongues* like 16-year-old boys look at a BMW.

"How did the boat get named *Two Tongues*?" Chad asked.

Sandy smiled at Trip and told his familiar tale, "Well, if ladies or kids are aboard, I answer that question by saying that Miguel speaks Spanish, and I speak English, so we have two tongues on the boat. Isn't that right, Miguel?"

Miguel looked at them and smiled, "Sí, señor."

"If it's just men, I answer their question with a question. Do you know why a dog licks his balls?"

Chad thought about it and answered no.

"Because he can," Sandy quipped. He gave a quick laugh and continued, "Two years ago, my buddy Doug and I won the million-dollar tarpon tournament. It was the third tournament we won that year, so we were on a roll. At the awards dinner, the announcer introduced me as a man that was luckier than a dog with two tongues. It made the paper, and I kinda liked it. So with the prize money we bought this boat and named it."

"A million-dollar tarpon tournament. What's that?" Chad asked in amazement.

"Tarpon fishing is big business for Boca Grande. Every summer the chamber of commerce sponsors eight weekly tournaments with the entry fee of $3,500 per boat. The field is limited to the first 100 boats to register. This produces a kitty of prize money of $350,000. First place gets 50%, second place 30%, and third place 20%. This is the format for the first seven tournaments. The season ending tournament is the million-dollar tournament. The chamber of commerce donates an additional $650,000 and this puts the kitty at a million and the same percentages apply. Only boats that fish all of the other tournaments can enter the million-dollar tournament. It's pretty wild in the pass during a tournament because everybody wants to be in the same place. Some-times the boats are so close, you have to push the other boats away with your feet. If another boat gets in the way and cuts off a hooked up tarpon, tempers flare."

Chad quickly did the math in his head, "You're telling me in eight weeks you made $850,000 in fishing tourna-ments?"

"Well, that was the total prize money. We had to pay taxes and I bought Miguel's wife a new minivan. We spent $3,500 in entrance fees in the other five tournaments and it takes $250 per day in gas to run the boat. Doug and I bought this boat together, and he gets a percentage of the yearly profits. But overall, it was a good summer!" Sandy said confidently.

Chad began to get angry when he realized that this care-free fishing captain made more money than he did. He also doubted if Sandy had ever been sued for 15 million dollars because of fishing malpractice.

"How many other tournaments have you won?" Chad asked.

"I won one other tournament 10 years ago. I've been second once, and third twice," Sandy reported.

Chad felt better knowing that Sandy had spent $28,000 per year in entrance fees for many years, without much success. However, he had to admit that Sandy's boat was appropriately named.

Chad enjoyed the ride as they headed north to Boca Grande pass. The sun was rising higher in the cloudless sky. Chad put suntan lotion on his fair skin as the boat slowed down off plane. Trip pointed to his left at Cayo Costa Island and told Chad it was state owned land that had been preserved as a state park. Australian pine trees stood tall in the middle of the island, rooted in the sand dunes. Between the Australian pines and the beach, palm trees provided cover for a wide variety of birds. As they went further north, they could see the hazy blue water rushing around the tip of the island into the Gulf. The strong outgoing tide seemed to please Sandy and Miguel. As the boat continued toward the middle of the pass, Chad saw the lighthouse on the tip of Gasparilla Island on the north shore. There were over 200 boats drifting the outgoing tide near the lighthouse.

Chad asked, "Why are all the boats there?"

"Look at the water between the boats as we get closer. You'll see." Sandy instructed.

The *Two Tongues* maneuvered to get in line with the other fishing boats. The other boats ranged in size from 17 feet to 60 feet. They all seemed to be drifting over a certain spot, and then going around the fleet and returning to the front of the line. Chad was watching the closest boat when he saw an explosion of water. Hundreds of tarpon leaped from the water and jumped a few feet into the air and then returned to the depths of the pass. He then looked around and saw six other schools of tarpon doing the same thing all around the boat, and he felt an adrenaline rush. These fish ranged in size from four feet to eight feet. Trip told Chad the world record was 305 pounds, and Chad suddenly realized that this wasn't going to be a relaxing day, sitting in the sun, drinking beer, and lazily holding a fishing rod.

Chad asked, "Why are they jumping?"

Miguel said with a smile, "Because they're happy."

Sandy instructed, "Tarpon can breathe through their mouth and through their gills. They gulp air when they come up and let it loose as they swim. Look overboard and you can see the bubbles."

Chad was ready to hook up and feel the power of these fish. Miguel was busy scrambling on the deck arranging the different rods in the right position. Sandy instructed Chad and Trip to go to the rear of the boat with each one at the opposite side. Miguel handed them the rods and waited on Sandy's directions. Sandy climbed up the tower and assumed the controls there. He was able to see all of the boat traffic and where the schools of fish were moving.

Sandy shouted down to Miguel, "Put on squirrelfish; we're going to try deep first.

After Miguel baited the hooks, Sandy said to Chad and Trip, "Gentlemen, we're in water that is 45 foot deep. The weights on the line will take the bait to the bottom. Go ahead and let out the line. Once it hits bottom, turn the reel two cranks off of bottom. When we hit the trench, let more line out until it hits bottom. It should be another 15-20 feet down. Reel up two cranks when it hits bottom."

Chad asked, "What's the trench?"

Sandy patiently explained as he looked through his polarized sunglasses at his depth finder, "About one half mile off of the lighthouse is a trench that's about a quarter mile long and about 50 yards wide that's at a 45-degree angle to shore. It's about 15 feet to 20 feet deeper than the surrounding area. Over the years, the current has eaten into the limestone ledge and produced sort of an underwater canyon. The tarpon that are in the canyon are out of the main current and ready to eat. They wait there and look up and see what the current has brought them for dinner. Most of the tarpon you see jumping are playin' and conductin' some sort of mating ritual before they head offshore to spawn."

Chad was holding onto his rod waiting for a bite. He again saw the school of tarpon jump out of the water and head back to the deep, hidden bottom. The tarpon were jumping so close to the boat, water got splashed on Chad.

He asked, "How can I tell when they bite?"

Miguel laughed.

Sandy smiled and said, "You'll know. We should be over the trench in just a minute. Look! The boats in front of us are hooked up."

Chad looked over at the boats and saw the other anglers

holding their poles bent into a shape that looked like an upside down "U." Suddenly, he saw a silver missile shoot up from the water. The hooked tarpon turned, twisted, and shook its head so hard, Chad could hear its gills rattle.

He heard angry profanities shouted from the second boat. Apparently, the second tarpon had broken the line.

Chad noticed a brunette on a third boat that was wearing a bikini bottom and no top. He was admiring the view when his rod slammed into the railing. Although he was hanging onto the rod with all his strength, line was being stripped off of his reel so fast it was creating a high pitched noise that sounded like a machine gun.

Miguel yelled to Sandy in the tower, "Hookup! Hook-up!"

Chad yelled, "Help! Holyshit! What do I do?"

Sandy yelled, "Hang on! I'll help you with the boat."

Sandy instructed Trip to reel in his line so it wouldn't get tangled with Chad's. He maneuvered the boat so the line was directly behind the boat. Sandy then put his boat into reverse and chased the fleeing tarpon. The other guides moved out of the way according to local custom.

Chad had never felt such strength before. He'd grown up riding and handling horses, and it felt like a dozen horses were attached to his line. Over 150 yards had been stripped from his reel, and he could see the bare spool under the few remaining yards of line.

Fortunately, the *Two Tongues* started to even out the battle. Miguel walked behind Chad and wrapped a fighting belt around his waist, fastened with Velcro. Chad put the butt of the rod in the holder to give him better leverage. The boat caught up to the tarpon and Chad was able to reel in half of the line. The battle was now in a stalemate with a tug-of-war. Chad would pull on the rod and reel in 10 yards, then the tarpon would take out 10 yards. This continued for 45 minutes.

Chad's arms were shaking with exhaustion, and the sun was getting hotter by the minute. The early morning breeze had stopped, and the Florida humidity was draining. Chad's clothes were dripping with sweat. He secretly hoped the tarpon would break his line and he'd be free from the torture. Then he noticed his line zipping through the water, coming to the surface.

Miguel yelled, "He's going to jump."

Chad was amazed at the speed with which the fish rose from the depths. He felt the line tighten and saw the water explode. A seven-foot tarpon launched himself into a twisting, flipping jump 15 feet into the air. When he landed, he ran sideways to the boat. The tarpon started to circle the boat and make quick, short darts. It was fighting differently than it had earlier. The tarpon was even more frantic as the fight continued. Suddenly, the fight stopped and there was no pulling on the line. At first, Chad cursed the line, thinking it had broken. When he started to reel in, he felt some weight on the end of the line, but it was not fighting. As the line was coming to the surface, he could see something silver on the end. It popped to the surface, and it took Chad a second to process what he was seeing. It was a bloody tarpon head, severed from the body.

Miguel shouted to Sandy, "A shark got him! It was a big tarpon; do you think it was Hitler?"

"What the hell is Hitler?" Chad asked. He was exhausted, and he felt the shark had cheated him.

Sandy yelled from the tower, "I'll come down and tell you. Miguel, grab us some beers."

Sandy climbed down from the tower and assumed the controls in the shade on the lower level. They all opened their beers. Sandy turned the boat around and headed back uptide, to the front of the line. He had to go slow so the wake of the *Two Tongues* didn't rock the smaller boats fishing.

As they cruised back, Sandy said, "Hitler is a 20-foot hammerhead shark that has been spotted in the pass for the past 40 years. Tarpon are the favorite food for hammerheads, and they follow the tarpon when they migrate to the pass. Most hammerheads that eat tarpon are 8 to 12 feet and anything over 14 feet is rare."

Sandy took a healthy drink of his beer before he continued. "I've seen Hitler twice in my life. The first time was when I was a boy. I was drifting the pass with my dad, and we were watching an older couple fight a big tarpon in a small boat. When they got it to the boat, the husband was holding the tarpon by his mouth and lifting it partially out of the water for a picture. The wife was focusing the camera, and Hitler came up out of the water and swallowed the 5-foot tarpon whole, and bit down on the man's arm. He lost his left hand and arm to the elbow.

"I remember my dad driving our boat over, jumping in their boat, and helping the man by tying a rope around the arm to stop the bleeding. The wife was yelling and crying hysterically. They got in our boat, and we towed their boat to the marina. I remember the man looking at his stub and not saying anything; he just looked at it. The man lived, but he and his wife moved to Nebraska."

Sandy checked his depth finder and looked at the other boats in the drifting fleet. He seemed pleased to see a school of thirty tarpon roll on the top of the water and flip their tales. The *Two Tongues* rode against the tide, motoring towards the front of the line for another drift as other boats fought tarpon.

Sandy continued, "The second time I saw Hitler was about five years ago, when I was fishin' a charter. A young dentist from Tampa, his wife, and their golden retriever, Betsy. We jumped three tarpon, but had lost 'em all. The wife liked to fish more than the dentist, and she was mad that

110

she hadn't boated any of them. She finally got a nice tarpon on and fought it to the boat. It took 'bout an hour, and we were getting the camera ready when Hitler showed up and cruised by the side of the boat with his dorsal fin five feet in the air. He swam by and then turned back toward her fish. She started yellin' at the shark to leave her tarpon alone. She gets mad and throws her Coke can at Hitler. It landed between the tarpon and Hitler, and Betsy jumps overboard after the damn can!

"Hitler turned on his side and swam toward the dog. Betsy never stopped swimming toward the can, until Hitler bit down on her. We could hear Betsy yelpin' under the bloody water. Hitler swam by the back of the boat with her hind legs and tail hangin' from the corner of his mouth, like he's showin' off. He went deep, and we didn't see him again. The lady lost it. I heard she had to be put in the hospital and medicated."

The men finished their beers in silence. Sandy brought the boat back around to the front of the fleet to begin another drift and went back up to the tower to scout for more schools of tarpon.

Sandy yelled down to Miguel, "The tide's faster now. Let's try crabs."

Miguel baited the rods with crabs and gave them to Trip and Chad. On Sandy's signal, they lowered their baits to the bottom. Both of them had tarpon take the bait on the way down and confusion was rampant as both fish immediately jumped. Chad's fish threw the hook loose, but Trip had a solid hookup. Thirty minutes later, they released a four-footer.

They jumped three other tarpon and boated a second during the day of fishing. At three in the afternoon, a thunderstorm threatened them from the east. They cut the fishing short and headed back to Cabbage Key. Both Chad and Trip were glad they were finished for the day because their bodies ached from fighting tarpon and their dehydration required cold beer from the bar.

Chapter 14

Al met Don for breakfast at the Cracker Barrel by Interstate 85 to discuss the problems caused by Dr. Elsworth and Fast Eddie, his media-hound lawyer. The meeting lasted an hour with Don criticizing every idea Al had brought up. He said they were either illegal, unethical, or both. Al was getting angry with Don, when he realized that Don was trying his best to figure out an answer. Don's problem was he was used to playing by the rules of the legal profession. Al realized Don had never dealt with the emotions caused by the dilemma of kill or be killed. Al looked into Don's eyes and saw the eyes of a scared man, desperate to solve the problem, within the bounds of the law. He could see that Don didn't have what it took to solve problems at any cost. However, his eagerness could be used, if needed.

Al knew that Dr. Elsworth and Fast Eddie had to be stopped before their third-party lawsuit became a story in the media. This would cause the stock price to drop, and they would lose all their money. Not to mention possible be arrested. If Al's family lost their money, people would die. Al started to analyze how Fast Eddie was going to produce evidence of their conspiracy. He correctly surmised there would be no other doctors testifying with Dr. Elsworth because they didn't want to lose their share of the HMO pie. Other doctors knew of LAMPCO's claims practices, but none of them wanted to risk losing the majority of their income.

Dr. Elsworth was going to testify about his past experiences with LAMPCO, and he would be the only witness. Fast Eddie would subpoena the records of LAMPCO to show how many claims had been denied. Dr. Elsworth could review these other medical claims that had been denied and testify they were reasonable and necessary claims. If Dr. Elsworth didn't testify about his experience on the Martin case and other cases, they couldn't prove their RICO claims. The records of LAMPCO might create questions, but without a doctor's testimony, they didn't matter. LAMPCO had their hired gun, Dr. Bennete, to give his expert opinion that all denied claims were proper.

Al suddenly realized the solution to his problem. If Dr. Elsworth was dead, Fast Eddie didn't have the witness he needed. No other doctors had the financial pressure of an uninsured medical malpractice claim hanging over their head. Therefore, Fast Eddie wouldn't find another doctor willing to risk his income. Al's conscience didn't bother him over this deadly solution; his only concern was how he could get away with it.

Al first had to find out Dr. Elsworth's schedule to arrange an accident. He called his favorite private investigator to learn Dr. Elsworth's habits and normal travel routes. Six hours later, the investigator called back with the news that Dr. Elsworth was recently served with divorce papers and spending a week tarpon fishing in Florida.

Al's plan was starting to come into focus. He'd call his cousins in Philadelphia to find out the name of a hit man in Miami and let him arrange an accident for Dr. Elsworth. After Fast Eddie's star witness was killed, he'd have very little evidence to prove the RICO claim. Al knew Fast Eddie's reputation for a fast buck and he would use this to get rid of him after his star witness was dead. Al would strongly suggest to Don Welch that his law firm, Prince and Wilson, hire Fast Eddie as a partner with a large signing bonus. Since Prince and Wilson represented LAMPCO, Fast Eddie would have to resign as counsel for the late Dr. Elsworth because of a conflict of interest. Fast Eddie would accept the offer for two reasons. The first reason was he had no case without a witness, and therefore, no chance of collecting a large contingency fee. The second, and most important reason, was the large signing bonus paid immediately upon withdrawing from the late Dr. Elsworth's case.

No other lawyer would take over the RICO case because the material witness was dead. Dr. Elsworth's widow wouldn't pay any lawyer to vindicate his name because she didn't care since she was divorcing him. LAMPCO would offer some nuisance money, with a provision in the settlement papers for confidentiality, to the Martin family and Karen Senard. The lawsuit would settle and never become public knowledge. Al was pleased with himself because he had solved the problem.

Chapter 15

As the *Two Tongues* docked at Cabbage Key, the thunderstorm rapidly approached from the east. Sandy could feel the temperature drop about 20 degrees and smelled the rain. The local duck population was waddling across the island looking for shelter. The dark line of low clouds let loose with a barrage of lightening that bounced off the water in the distance. Everyone on the docks started running towards the restaurant.

Sandy told Miguel, "We're gonna wait out the storm here. Do you want to come inside with us?"

Miguel replied, "No, I'll clean the inside of the boat and wait here."

Sandy, Trip, and Chad hurried off the boat and up the shell mound to the restaurant. The first drops of rain hit their backs as they opened the door and entered the restaurant. They walked through the restaurant and went to the bar.

Sandy looked around the dimly lit bar as his eyes adjusted to the change. He smiled, approached a couple at the end of the bar, and said, "Rob, how are you and your pretty wife doing?"

"Sandy, where have you been? I haven't seen you in months. Where have you been hiding?" Rob Wells asked.

Sandy replied, "I've been fishing every day since tarpon season started. We've been killin' 'em the past two weeks. I came in with my charter early because of the storm. They're staying here on the island with you. Let me introduce you— this is Trip and Chad. They're two doctors out of Atlanta. Trip and Chad, this is Rob Wells and his wife Phyllis. They're the owner/operators of Cabbage Key."

Rob and Phyllis shook hands with Trip and Chad.

Rob said to the bartender, "Nate, could you bring us all a round of drinks?"

Nate took their order, and Sandy reported on their day of fishing, "We had six tarpon on and boated two. The first one we had on was a seven-footer. Chad fought him for 'bout an hour until a shark got 'em. Nothin' but a head left. Isn't that right Chad?"

Chad answered, "It was the biggest fish I've ever seen. Miguel thinks it might've been Hitler."

Rob asked, "Hitler? No one's seen him for two years. What do you think Sandy?"

Sandy said, "I don't know. The shark had to be big. We didn't get a look at 'em though."

Rob said, "The last time I heard of anyone seeing him was off the sea buoy, near the elbow of the channel. A couple of flats boats had anchored and started a chum line

118

for tarpon. They were hoping to get a bunch of tarpon feeding and then try to catch 'em on a flyrod. They jumped one tarpon before Hitler showed up. All of the tarpon sounded, and Hitler followed the chum line right up to the flats boats. It scared 'em so bad one guy pissed in his pants."

Sandy said, "Last week, Bobby was out with a charter and gut-hooked a manta- ray. It was eight feet long and six feet wide. While he was holding it up at the edge of the boat for camera shots, three hammerheads about seven to eight feet long swam up and attacked the bleeding manta-ray. It scared his charters so bad, they asked to go back to the dock."

Sandy and Rob traded more fishing stories and caught up with the local gossip about new real estate development on Pine Island. Phyllis, ever the good hostess, asked Trip and Chad about Atlanta. They talked about the Braves and the new restaurants and clubs in Atlanta. Trip and Chad were glad to be out of the sun and off the boat. Their arm muscles ached every time they raised their beers. After a few minutes of conversation, Phyllis excused herself to help plan dinner.

Sandy asked Chad, "What did you think about your first day of salt water fishing?"

Chad said, "It was better than I could've imagined. It was a bonus that I got to see firsthand what Hitler could do."

Chad was developing a sense of pride that he'd encountered living, local history at the end of his fishing line. "Are there any other legends I should know about?"

Sandy exhaled his cigarette smoke slowly and said, "I'm sure you've heard of Blackbeard the Pirate. His name was José Gaspar, but he called himself Gasparilla. His home base was Boca Grande. That's why they named it Gasparilla Island. He raided the Spanish ships for treasure and women he could hold for ransom. As you can imagine, virgins were worth more than non-virgins.

"Captiva Island is about 12 miles south of Boca Grande. Back then, Captiva and Upper Captiva were one island until a hurricane around the turn of the century split them into two. Captiva is Spanish for 'captive' and Gasparilla kept all of the virgins on Captiva, so his men wouldn't reduce the value of his ransom. His older, trusted mates guarded the virgins, so even if the young bucks decided to row a rowboat to Captiva, they were too tired to do anything. The non-virgins stayed with Gasparilla and his men for their pleasure. He was killed on his boat in 1886 in a fight with a U.S. Navy ship off the coast."

Sandy finished his drink and said amusingly, "Of course, there haven't been any virgins on Captiva since then."

The group laughed and ordered another round of drinks. Rob slipped behind the bar and brought out Cuban cigars for everyone. Everybody lit up and enjoyed the sweet aroma as the fishing stories continued throughout the afternoon happy hour. Chad excused himself to his room for a bathroom break. After he relieved himself, he took his afternoon amphetamine and thought about calling Fast Eddie's office on his cell phone to see if there were any developments on the case. He decided to go back and enjoy happy hour.

Rob and Sandy complained about the commercial fishermen that were illegally gillnetting. The local fishing had improved since the gillnetting ban had been in place. However, the netters were still netting at night. They discussed the best way to stop it and make the fishing even better. Rob talked about how the stone crab claws were bigger and more abundant this year. He had just finished checking the restaurant's new shipment for freshness and quality. After an hour and a half, the rain cleared and the sun came out. The 100% humidity returned and reminded everyone it was summer. Sandy made plans for the next day of fishing with Trip and Chad.

As Sandy stood up to leave, he said to the group, "I have a toast I'd like to make. Here's to livin' as long as you want, and wantin' as long as you live!"

The group laughed and raised their drinks to the toast.

Sandy walked toward the door and said, "I'll pick ya'll up at eight. Don't be too hung over!"

Trip and Chad continued to drink with Rob. There was no one else in the bar, except a Hispanic man sitting by himself in the corner, next to the dormant fireplace, reading a magazine. He'd been there during the entire happy hour, drinking ice water. And listening.

Chapter 16

Carlos Rameriz enjoyed killing people. He learned how to do it as a U.S. Army Ranger and had been doing it for profit for the past 16 years. Carlos was born in the poor section of Miami; his parents emigrated from Havana in the fifties when Castro came to power. They were farmers and had no marketable skills in Miami, so his father worked as a janitor and his mother as a maid. Carlos was determined to be rich when he became an adult.

Carlos had three older brothers who were constantly fighting with him. He was the shortest and thinnest, so his nickname was "runt." As a teenager, he took up boxing in local tournaments with the dream of getting rich as a champion. He had an average record as a boxer. He couldn't control his height, but his devotion to fitness produced a chiseled body. Carlos continued fighting as a lightweight because he loved the combat. From 17 to 21 he boxed an amateur match every month. This grueling schedule produced a win-loss record of 31 and 17, nine broken noses, three cracked teeth, and a periodic ringing in his left ear.

At 21, he realized his desire to fight was stronger than

his skill in the ring. He looked around the boxing club and saw all the washed-out boxers that would hang around the gym because they had nothing better to do. He decided he was going to enlist in the Army and get paid to fight.

Carlos excelled in basic training and his supervisors picked him to be part of the Rangers, an elite division of the Army that specialized in clandestine warfare and special operations. Carlos discovered special operations meant destroying property and killing people in foreign countries that weren't public knowledge to the average American. He learned how to infiltrate enemy countries with a small group and cause havoc. His group was responsible for damaging key strategic outposts in enemy countries. While serving as a Ranger, he killed 16 men in unofficial combat in foreign countries and six of them he only used his hands as weapons.

Carlos served in the Army for five years without any problems. However, his testosterone finally got him in trouble. His unit commander always selected Carlos for the most difficult job on a mission, and Carlos enjoyed the challenge. He didn't realize that discrimination was the reason he was chosen. One night Carlos couldn't sleep while on his home base and took a walk. He was near the Officer's Club when he saw, from a distance, his commander standing outside with a buddy.

Carlos overheard his commander talking in a loud, drunken voice. "That goddamn Cuban is like a cat; he has nine lives! He should've been killed with all the shit I had 'im doing. I guess I'll keep givin' him the shit jobs until he catches a bullet, because no one will miss him. He probably doesn't even know who his father really is. They all breed like animals."

Carlos ran toward his commander and yelled, "What the hell are you talking about?"

His drunken commander looked at him and laughed. "What are you doing back here? Are you done screwing your sister?"

Carlos exchanged punches with both of them until other officers came out and separated them. When the fight was over, both Carlos and his commander were taken to the hospital. Carlos was dishonorably discharged and went back to Miami. His depression worsened, and he started drinking heavily. After six months of drinking and feeling sorry for himself, Carlos woke up one morning and decided he was tired of being broke and homeless. He decided to start his own business and make some money. He knew how to fight and how to kill, and he already tried unsuccessfully to make money at fighting. He decided to make money killing people.

Carlos approached some of his old neighborhood friends that were involved in crime. He told them of his training and that he was starting a new career. Carlos killed efficiently and quietly, and his ruthless reputation grew in the criminal community. After his drinking binge when he was discharged from the Army, Carlos never drank again. Because of this and his 100% killing success rate, his nickname in the Miami underworld was "Iceman."

One of Carlos' regular customers put him in touch with Al Brognese. Al flew down from Atlanta and met with Carlos at the Miami Dog Track, since they both enjoyed betting on dogs. They sat in the lounge and ordered drinks, Al a martini and Carlos a bottle of Evian.

Carlos asked Al, "What's your favorite bet?"

Al replied, "I watch the dogs when they parade 'em before they're put in the starter gate. I bet on the ones that take a shit; I know I'd run faster if I'd just taken a dump. I bet $10 each to win, place, and show."

Al lit his Partagas robusto cigar and asked Carlos, "What about you? What's your bet?"

Carlos replied, "I don't bet every race. I only bet when there's a long shot of 50 to 1 or higher. When there's a long shot still on the odds board 2 minutes or less before the race, I wheel the dog on trifectas. I wheel him to win, place, and show."

Al smiled and said, "That's a very expensive bet. Does it pay off?"

Carlos replied, "Not usually. But when it does, it usually pays between $3,000 and $5,000 on a $126 bet."

After four races, Al had won $40 and Carlos hadn't

made a bet. They agreed to take a walk and strolled down to a secluded area of the terrace next to the track.

Al said, "You come highly recommended, Mr. Rameriz. I have a problem with a doctor out of Atlanta that has information that could hurt my company, and I need him to die in an accident. He's fishing over on the West Coast at a place called Cabbage Key. Do you think you could arrange an accident? It has to look like an accident."

Carlos said, "A lot of boating accidents have occurred in Miami over the years. Especially since I got out of the Army. Accidents are not cheap. I need $100,000 wired to my Swiss account before I begin. After the job is complete, wire me the other $100,000."

Al nodded slowly and looked at the dogs being loaded into the starting gate. "No problem. Give me the information and it'll be done first thing tomorrow. The doctor is only going to be at Cabbage Key until the end of the week. Can you get it done?"

Carlos replied, "Of course. I'll give you my account number and my e-mail address. When the money is transferred, send me an e-mail that the money has been sent. I don't use phones for communicating; there are too many people listening."

Al gave Carlos the private investigator's report and a picture of Dr. Elsworth. Al got his account number and e-mail address from Carlos and returned to Atlanta. The next morning, Al told the Chief Financial Officer at LAMPCO that he hired a new advertising consultant and needed $200,000 to retain him. The first $100,000 was transferred to Switzerland by 10:00 a.m.

Chapter 17

Carlos received his e-mail message from Al at 10:02
Monday morning while at his rented condo on Miami Beach.
He accessed his Swiss bank account through the bank's
website and confirmed the money was in his account. He
grabbed his suitcase, already packed with clothes, and his
duffel bag, packed with deadly supplies, and headed west
across the state to Cabbage Key. He'd made calls the night
before to find out about the access to and from Cabbage Key,
and he'd made different plans based on the weather condi-
tions.

He drove across Alligator Alley and arrived in Ft. Myers by two in the afternoon. After he realized it was good
weather, he chose to go onto Captiva Island to rent a boat because there were more tourists on Captiva, and he'd blend in
better. If the weather had been windy, he would have gone
to Pine Island for a shorter crossing, but he'd stand out more
because there were fewer tourists on Pine Island. He traveled through Ft. Myers and crossed over the causeway onto
Sanibel Island. He drove slowly on the tourist packed roads
until he crossed the Blind Pass Bridge onto Captiva Island,

which was as far as he could travel by land.

Carlos' phone calls and research convinced him to rent a boat from Jenson's Marina at the northern end of Captiva on the bay side. Carlos parked his car under a coconut palm and unloaded his gear. He filled out the rental paperwork and paid with cash. He loaded the 16-foot boat with his gear and headed north to Cabbage Key while looking at his classic road map. It didn't show all of the shallow areas, and he ran aground twice on submerged sandbars. It took him two hours to find Cabbage Key, and the dock master directed him to the end of the west dock. He rented a room and unloaded his gear.

After a quick shower, Carlos walked from his room down to the bar where he asked the bartender, Nate, how long it would be before the fishing boats came in, because he was interested in chartering a boat. Nate told him normally around four, but earlier if there were afternoon thunderstorms. Carlos ordered an Evian water and went back to his room to wait.

He unpacked his clothes and arranged his gear. He had just finished organizing everything when he heard approaching thunder. He went down to the bar with a magazine and ordered another Evian and ice. He had been sitting in the corner by the unlit fireplace for about five minutes when Dr. Chadwick Elsworth III, his friend, and the fishing guide came into the bar.

Carlos sat and listened to their ridiculous fishing stories and jokes. He watched them poison their bodies with alcohol and smoke. It was boring, but necessary to gather the information for a successful job. Carlos had to put his hand over his mouth to hide his smile when the guide said he would pick them up at eight the next morning. When the guide left the bar, Carlos gave him a two-minute head start and then followed him down to the dock, where he looked admiringly at the *Two Tongues*. It was a pity to blow up such a beautiful boat.

Carlos went back to his room and rearranged his bomb supplies after seeing the size of the *Two Tongues*. He checked and double-checked everything. He laid out his clothes for the next day and packed everything else.

He walked down the hall to the bar and asked Nate if he could pay because he was leaving early the next morning. He paid in cash and went back to his room where he ate two apples and a granola bar while he finalized his plan. He looked at his equipment one last time and went over his plan again. He took a warm shower, dried off in front of the window air conditioning unit, and relaxed as he lay down in his bed. He was just another businessman resting before his big job. He debated whether he'd spend his next vacation in Europe or the South Pacific. He set his alarm and read *Fortune* magazine for an hour before he went to sleep.

The next morning Carlos woke up five minutes before

his alarm went off at 5:30 a.m. He lay still in bed and went over his plan again in his head. The alarm finally went off and he jumped out of his bed, rested and ready to complete his job. He showered, packed his remaining toiletries, and loaded his luggage and gear on his boat. He had all of his gear organized in the boat by 6:45 a.m.

Carlos waited until no one was on the docks and put on his snorkeling gear, grabbed his dive bag, and quietly slipped off the rear of his boat. He swam down to the end of the dock and hid behind a large sailboat. He grabbed hold of a rope hanging off the sailboat and waited for the *Two Tongues*. As Carlos waited in the water, small snappers swam up to his legs and nipped at his abundant, dark hair as the tide moved it. The water movement caused the snapper to mistake his hair for small baitfish.

Sandy pulled into the Cabbage Key channel at 7:50 a.m. As he approached the dock, Miguel threw the ropes to the dock master, Terry, and he secured the *Two Tongues*. Chad and Trip were 20 minutes late because of their hangovers. Sandy laughed at them as they slowly walked down the dock. Sandy knew from experience that a night of drinking and telling fish stories with Rob made for a rough morning.

Sandy asked, "Would either of you like a beer? How about some whiskey shots?"

Trip replied, "I'm never going to drink again. And I swear I mean it this time."

132

Chad just rolled his eyes as he stepped on the boat as Miguel untied the ropes.

Carlos had waited for the *Two Tongues* to dock at Cabbage Key. He took a deep breath and quietly sank to the bottom. He swam underwater, directly under the dock, to the *Two Tongues*. He came up for air underneath the dock, next to the secured *Two Tongues*, and then swam quietly under it.

The boat looked completely different from underwater. The bottom was painted with a black protective paint. There were two inboard engines that powered the boat. About two-thirds of the way toward the back of the boat, two stainless steel shafts emerged from the boat. These stainless steel shafts ran parallel to the boat and had brass propellers on the end. About eighteen inches behind these propellers were bronze rudders that turned the boat. These rudders were directly under the rear of the boat and about three feet underwater.

Carlos remembered at the rear of the boat, water level, there was a wooden platform. This was a dive platform that extended about three feet behind the boat and ran the entire width of the boat. It was used to stand on to pull divers out of the water. Directly above the dive platform, *Two Tongues* was spelled out in 18-inch gold and black letters.

Carlos swam to the back of the boat and came up toward the rudders. He pulled plastic explosives and a remote detonator from his dive bag and secured them on the rear of the boat, about a foot underwater, directly beneath the dive platform. He used enough plastic explosives to blow up a bridge because he wanted to make sure there would be no survivors and the evidence would sink to the bottom.

Carlos swam back to his boat and threw his empty dive bag and snorkeling gear in the rear. He looked around and made sure no one was nearby, and then pulled himself into the boat. He put a shirt on, took a bottle of Evian out of the cooler, and sat waiting on the *Two Tongues* to go fishing. He put the transmitter for the detonation device next to his seat.

Carlos watched as Dr. Elsworth and his friend got on the boat and wondered what they'd eaten for their last meal. Carlos followed the *Two Tongues* to Boca Grande Pass and waited for the boat to get in the middle of the fishing fleet. He wanted plenty of witnesses for this terrible accident.

Chapter 18

The *Two Tongues* slowed as it headed toward the group of boats drifting the pass. As they approached, Sandy picked up the transmitter on his VHF radio and said, "That's my buddy Doug over in that yellow boat. Looks like each of his friends has a tarpon on."

Sandy pushed the transmit button for his radio and said, "Doug, come back. This is the *Two Tongues*. We're coming up behind you."

Doug picked up his radio transmitter and answered, "Good morning, Sandy. Where have you been? They've been biting for the past 45 minutes. Everybody in the pass is hooked up."

Sandy replied, "My charters had to get their beauty sleep this morning. A whiskey storm hit 'em last night at Cabbage Key. Good luck with the fish. 10-4."

"10-4," Doug signed off.

Doug Shearer was a year younger than Sandy. He was a fourth generation native of Matlacha. He and Sandy had played football on rival high school teams where they both excelled. Doug, who played linebacker, often bragged about tackling Sandy after he caught the ball as wide receiver. Sandy bragged about catching balls and running by Doug for touchdowns. They were both good enough to get scholarships to Florida State where they became best friends.

At Florida State class work was easy for Doug, and he always had good grades. Sandy had to work twice as hard at class work as everyone else to get average grades. Doug got into the habit of helping Sandy study for his tests, and Sandy's grades became better. One fall afternoon during their sophomore year, Sandy came busting into Doug's dorm room and said, "I got an A in English with Professor Franklin. It's the first time I ever got an A in my life. Let's go celebrate at the Big Still."

Doug replied, "That's great you got an A, but I don't know about the Big Still though. It's a rough place."

Sandy said, "Don't worry, everybody there just wants to have fun. I know this waitress from Denny's, and she tells me all her friends go there, and they love football players. Come on, let's leave these little prissy college girls and go find some good southern women."

Doug reluctantly agreed, and they left in Sandy's Ford pickup. They drove to the north side of Tallahassee and pulled into the parking lot of the Big Still. It was an old department store that had gone out of business and had been recently converted into the biggest country bar in Tallahassee. Most bars in Tallahassee catered to the college crowd.

However, the Big Still advertised itself as the "working man's bar," and a rough crowd was the result.

Doug and Sandy went inside and sat at the bar as the large speakers boomed "It's a Family Tradition" by Hank Williams, Jr. The regulars looked disapprovingly at the two muscular college boys wearing Florida State t-shirts and shorts. A few beers later, Sandy's waitress friend from Denny's came in with three of her friends. Sandy and Doug walked over to their table, getting hostile glares from the regulars.

Sandy said, "Hi Darlene. This is my friend Doug."

Darlene said, "Hi there, good looking. These are my friends Betty, Candy, and Myra."

Doug and Sandy sat down with their newfound friends, who were all divorced, chain-smoking, and wore enough make-up to rival Tammy Faye Baker. Darlene hit it off with Doug and was sitting in his lap after two margaritas. The other three were fighting over Sandy. Unfortunately, Darlene's ex-husband was across the bar playing pool and drinking heavily. He watched his ex-wife flirting with the young college man and got angrier by the minute.

When Sandy went to the bathroom, Darlene's ex-husband and five of his construction worker friends approached Doug. Darlene's ex-husband walked up, grabbed Darlene by the hair, pulled her off Doug, and said, "Woman, you don't come into my bar and start acting like a whore."

Doug jumped up and said, "Let her go."

The ex-husband and two of his friends ran at Doug and tackled him. The fight was mostly one-sided as they held Doug on the ground and beat him. When Sandy came out of the bathroom, he saw the brawl and ran over. The other three friends of the ex-husband tackled Sandy and pushed him toward the door. One pulled a 9-inch Bowie knife out and said, "Boy, 'less you want some more holes in ya body, you better wait outside for ya friend."

Sandy looked at the glistening knife, then over the man's shoulder and saw Doug being beaten senseless. He turned and ran outside to his truck where he had his 12-gauge shotgun hanging across his rear window. He opened up the glove compartment and only found one shell. They had gone hunting the prior weekend and used all the other ammunition, so he loaded the single shell and ran back into the Big Still. As soon as he ran into the front door, he fired the shotgun at the ceiling. Everything got real quiet and the beating of Doug stopped as they looked up. Sandy ran toward the group with the gun pointed at them.

Sandy bluffed with his unloaded gun and yelled, "All right boys. I'm ready to go to hell or jail. Any of you pussies wanna go with me?"

No one moved, and Sandy yelled to Doug, "Come on, let's go."

Doug staggered to his feet and wiped the blood from

his nose and mouth as he limped toward Sandy. They made a quick exit and headed for the hospital. Doug had a deep cut on his right cheek that required 84 stitches and a broken nose. The bruises healed, but the cut left a three-inch scar on Doug's right cheek.

Doug got his degree in criminology, returned to Matlacha and joined the Lee County Sheriff's Department. He started as a road deputy and was promoted rapidly through the ranks because of his talent and hard work. For the past six years, he had been a senior detective working on major crimes. Sandy and Doug fished together at least twice a month. Every summer Doug used his vacation time to fish all the tarpon tournaments with Sandy. Doug had dated Sandy's younger sister, Amanda, for eight years after he returned from Florida State. She broke off the relationship because she decided she didn't want to be married to a cop. She moved to Sarasota and married a real estate developer. Doug was totally despondent after the breakup, and Sandy had been there for him in his dark time, which Doug never forgot.

Doug was five feet, 10 inches tall and kept in shape by jogging and swimming. He had wavy, dark brown hair and green eyes. He told everyone the three-inch scar on his right cheek was from a football injury. Doug dated a lot but never married. He saw the divorce rate among his fellow officers, combined this observation with his hurt psyche from Amanda, and ran from serious relationships.

He loved his job because he felt he was making the world a better place by outsmarting the bad guy. He had solved many cases that others couldn't, and between his long hours as a detective and his passion for fishing, he didn't have much free time. He liked it that way because it seemed that whenever he had a girlfriend, she complained he either worked too much or fished too much. He made it clear to them that he was too old to change, and they either understood or they broke up. Doug had many acquaintances, but he only had a few friends, and Sandy was his best one.

Doug was looking at the *Two Tongues* maneuver to get in line for the proper drift through the pass. Suddenly, he saw a bright orange flash that instantly covered the *Two Tongues*. The deafening sound of the explosion momentarily followed the sight of the erupting fire. Doug instinctively turned his head away and fell to the deck of his boat.

Doug jumped up and looked back to where the *Two Tongues* was seconds before. There was only sickening black smoke and some debris burning brightly. He could see debris falling from the sky and splashing into the water all around his boat. He flinched when he heard something hit the deck of his boat. He looked down and saw a bloody shoe with a severed foot. He picked it up and saw it was a white Sperry boat shoe, the kind Sandy always wore.

As he realized what had happened, he stumbled to the

side of his boat and threw up until he had dry heaves. His friends on the boat cut their lines loose from the fighting tarpon and took over the controls. They powered Doug's boat over to the flaming hull, hoping for survivors in the water. The tower and cabin had blown apart, and the only thing that was recognizable was the stringers from the hull of the boat. The fiberglass coating was burning an unnatural, fluorescent green flame, and small pieces of the boat were floating next to the burning hull. They looked for survivors, but there was nothing but burning fuel in the water. After Doug got hold of himself, his cop mentality came back to him. He got on his marine radio and told all the other boats in the pass to look for survivors. He then radioed the Coast Guard, who took over the investigation.

After a thirty-minute search by all the boats, two shoes had been found and Miguel's hat. There were no other body parts found, but Doug continued driving through the pass looking for his friend's remains. The only thing he found and kept, that was identifiable, was part of the stern of the boat that had the letters "*Two T*" partially visible, even though the wood was burned. After a three-hour search, the Coast Guard called Doug on the radio and said they were calling off the search because they were sure everyone was dead.

Doug couldn't believe Sandy and his crew were vaporized by the blast. He felt an overwhelming need to find some remains to bury. He drove around the pass for another two hours looking for something. He couldn't imagine telling Sandy's father that he couldn't find a body. Doug's friends in the boat finally convinced him to leave the pass and go home. As they motored away from the pass, Doug's mind couldn't let go of the memory of the fiery explosion and the eardrum-piercing blast.

Sandy had always been meticulous with the maintenance of his boat, so Doug couldn't believe that there was defective wiring or a broken pump. Sandy always came into the marina on Thursday afternoons for his weekly maintenance of the *Two Tongues*. Doug tried to think rationally about what could've caused the explosion, but his emotions overcame him and he began to tear up. He let his friends drive his boat home to Matlacha while he cried uncontrollably.

Chapter 19

Fast Eddie was sitting in his Lazy-Boy at home watching Moneyline when the phone rang. It was his answering service with an emergency phone call from Sarah Elsworth. The answering service patched the telephone call through, and Fast Eddie listened to the terrible news of the explosion. Sarah Elsworth ended the conversation by asking Fast Eddie to refund any unused retainer her husband had paid him. Fast Eddie assured her the retainer was used up and he would make sure to send her a current bill for all money owed to him. Fast Eddie felt a chill run down his spine. He got up out of his recliner and quickly went around his house, locking the windows and doors. Eddie was standing in front of his TV thinking about Chad and the lawsuit when the phone rang, causing him to jump into the air. Fast Eddie answered his portable phone on the second ring.

Don Welch said, "Good evening, Mr. Palsky, this is Don Welch from Prince and Wilson. How are you doing tonight?"

Fast Eddie felt the hairs on the back of his neck stand up, and he quickly looked around the room and at the front door.

Eddie said, "I'm a little shook up. My client, Dr. Elsworth, was just blown up in a boating accident in Florida. We are, I mean, we were, suing your client, LAMPCO."

Don responded in his most solemn voice, "I heard on the radio, and it's a terrible thing. Our prayers at the firm go out to his family. I know this is a difficult time, but do you have a minute to talk?"

Fast Eddie could detect the false feeling of remorse, "I suppose, but first tell me how you got my home number. It's unlisted. Oh, and by the way, what radio station is reporting the explosion? I want to listen."

Don was flustered by the questions, but stumbled through a response, "Well, I, um, your number was given to me by one of my partners. And, uh, I don't remember which station, I heard it on my car radio. I'm sorry if I disturbed you. Should I call your office tomorrow?"

Fast Eddie's curiosity was piqued. "No, we can talk now. What's on your mind?"

Don cleared his throat and said, "Well, we just had our monthly partner's meeting tonight. Our firm has been swamped with litigation because we have three new insurance companies that we've picked up as clients this month. As you can imagine, there are a lot of cases in suit. We're making a lot of money, but we're falling behind. We need an experienced litigator, and your name came up. You've had some nice verdicts lately, and we're prepared to offer you a full partner's position starting immediately. Last year, the partners made $400,000 with a retirement plan and benefits. We're also prepared to offer you a $200,000 signing bonus and a firm car. You can choose between a Lexus and Mercedes."

Fast Eddie was flabbergasted. Prince and Wilson offering him a partnership was like IBM hiring Dennis Rodman as a spokesman. After a few seconds of silence, he managed to respond, "Well, Mr. Welch, your offer is a little unexpected. I'll have to think about it. When do you need an answer? Can I talk to my wife about it?"

Don responded, "Of course, but there is one housekeeping matter. You'll have to withdraw as counsel for the late Dr. Elsworth. He has sued LAMPCO, our client, so it would be a conflict of interest for you to represent him, or his estate, if you joined our firm. I don't want to hurry you, but we need an answer by tomorrow at noon, or we'll have to make other arrangements."

Suddenly, it made sense to Fast Eddie—they were trying to buy his silence. Fast Eddie said quietly, "I understand. Let me sleep on it, and I'll let you know by noon tomorrow. Good night."

Don said good night and hung up the phone. He felt like he needed a long shower to get the dirt off of him, but Al had reminded him there was a problem to solve, and this was not a case he wanted to risk losing. Don tried to imagine introducing Fast Eddie to his corporate clients and got a migraine headache.

Fast Eddie was confused. He knew they were trying to buy his silence because LAMPCO was responsible for Dr. Chadwick's death. Apparently, his idea of a third party lawsuit involving the RICO statute was right on point. LAMPCO wanted this lawsuit over at any price. The dollar signs started floating in his daydream as he imagined a ten million-dollar settlement and his 40% contingent fee.

He started thinking of how he would continue the lawsuit and get rich by exposing LAMPCO. After thirty minutes debating with himself, Fast Eddie realized he had no witnesses to present his case. He could cause a lot of noise by calling a press conference and blaming LAMPCO, but he couldn't prove it in court. They might even sue him for slander. More importantly, he couldn't make any more money representing Dr. Elsworth, or his estate.

Fast Eddie started thinking of the offer. He had graduated at the bottom of his class at law school. He had struggled over the past 25 years to build a profitable practice and had done eviction and bankruptcy cases for discount rates until his practice had grown. His last few years had produced some nice cases, but he had no retirement plan or rich corporate clients anxious to pay him to keep them out of trouble.

His best year in practice was last year when he had made $160,000, but with no retirement, car, or benefits. His worst year in practice he had made $30,000. He had never had an expense account or a corporate membership at a country club. He was tired of the hassles of running a sole proprietorship.

Fast Eddie thought of his wife and three daughters as he considered the lucrative offer Don Welch has just made him. His wife had stuck by him in the rough times and his daughters would all be in college soon. They all wanted convertibles and to attend a private college. Last week, he watched a news report that claimed private colleges cost an average of $15,000 a year. He figured four years per daughter and it came to $180,000. He thought of how happy his wife would be playing bridge at a country club while his daughters sunbathed by the pool. After he finished a round of golf, he could meet them in the clubhouse for a champagne lunch and charge his firm's expense account. He then mentally started spending the $200,000 signing bonus. He could pay off his business credit line, his credit cards, his equity line on his house, and still have enough left over for a new Volvo for his wife.

Fast Eddie also wondered what would happen to him if he declined the offer. If LAMPCO would kill a doctor, they would happily kill a lawyer. He called his wife on her cell phone while she driving to pick up their daughters from the movies.

She answered the phone, "Hello."

Fast Eddie announced proudly, "Honey, stop at the liquor store and get some champagne. We have something to celebrate."

Chapter 20

Once Doug returned by boat to his waterfront home in Matlacha, his mood changed. He was incensed his friend had died and was determined to find out why the boat exploded. He knew it was no accident, and the responsible party would be held accountable if it was the last thing he ever did. Doug called Miller's Marina where Sandy had docked his boat and had it serviced. The head marina mechanic, Ronnie, had heard the news and was extremely upset. He told Doug that he'd serviced the boat weekly since Sandy had bought it, and there were only two possible alternatives that could cause an accidental explosion.

The first alternative was that there was leaking gas in the engine, producing fumes that the blower pump didn't blow out of the engine room. If there was an overheated engine, it could produce a spark. The second alternative was there was some bad wiring that produced an electrical fire, and the gas in the boat was ignited.

Ronnie said the problem with both these scenarios is Sandy had the most modern alarm system on the market in the engine room. It registered fumes, smoke, and an overheated engine. The alarm system would've had to break at the same time another system failed for this explosion to occur without warning. Ronnie said it was very unlikely this would happen on a new boat that was serviced weekly. Doug thanked Ronnie for his help and hung up the phone. Ronnie had been at the marina for 20 years and was well respected, so he doubted there were problems with the service the boat received.

Doug walked out of his house into his backyard. His house was on a canal that emptied into the Matlacha River, and his twenty-foot boat, a ten-year old Mako center console, was tied up to his dock. It had taken his friends 30 minutes to drive him back from Boca Grande pass. The entire time Doug looked at the burnt wooden and fiberglass wreckage that had the letters "Two T" on it. He looked at it as a symbol of his dead friend. Now it was time to look at as evidence.

Doug tried to force his grief to the back of his mind as he concentrated on the evidence. He boarded his boat and looked at the cracked wood and fiberglass wreckage in the back of his boat. He thought it was odd that it was cracked from the painted outside side toward the inside of the boat. He also thought it was odd there were burn marks on the painted letters and not on the inside of the wreckage. If the explosion had come from the gas tank or the engine room, the force of the explosion would've pushed the rear of the boat away from the flash point. The burn should have been on the inside of the wooden and fiberglass pieces. It should've cracked from the inside out, producing jagged edges. The edge of the wood was angled totally opposite of how it should've been and Doug's cop brain started considering the possibilities.

He'd talked to Sandy seconds before he died, and there was nothing wrong with his boat. The two scenarios suggested by Ronnie would've caused problems with the boat a long time before an explosion. Sandy would've said something was wrong with his boat when he'd talked to him on the radio. The physical evidence, the rear piece of wood, didn't support either of the two scenarios. Doug needed more evidence to analyze.

The problem was that all of the evidence was either burnt up or at the bottom of Boca Grande pass. Doug could sense that something was not right, and he had to know the truth. He called the head of the Lee County Sheriff dive team and said he needed a boat, a crew, and an experienced diver to dive with him to the bottom of the pass. He explained that it was needed for tomorrow, and they'd have to dive at slack tide to avoid the strong and unpredictable currents. They made arrangements to meet at Pineland Marina the next morning at ten.

Doug was an experienced diver, but most of his dives had been in the 30 to 40 foot range on offshore wrecks.

He'd never dived to the bottom of the pass. In fact, he'd never heard of anyone diving the pass because it was treacherous and stupid to dive in such an environment. There were different currents at different levels in the pass. The hazy blue water also limited visibility. The Two Tongues was over the trench when it exploded. If there was any evidence, it was at the bottom, in a deep, dark underwater canyon. Doug spent the evening in his backyard, sitting on his seawall, watching the predator fish eating the small baitfish gathered around the lights on the docks and thinking about Sandy. At midnight, his exhaustion forced him inside for the night. He had problems sleeping, but finally fell asleep at 4:00 a.m.

He woke up to the sun shining through his window. He showered, ate a small breakfast, loaded up his dive gear, and drove to Pineland Marina. The dive crew and boat were already there when he pulled his truck up next to the dock.

Doug approached the boat and said, "Good morning, Sergeant Busbee. Are we ready for the dive?"

Sergeant Busbee said, "Doug, we're ready. But are you sure you want to dive the pass?"

Doug explained why he thought the explosion was suspicious. When he told them he had talked to Sandy moments before the explosion, he got choked up. When he regained his composure, he resumed his explanation of the evidence.

Sergeant Busbee explained he'd called the Coast Guard.

They were going to keep boats from fishing over the trench during their dive for evidence. Doug loaded his dive gear into the Sheriff's dive boat, and they left the marina. The twin 200-horsepower Mercury engines pushed the dive boat quickly across Pine Island Sound. Sergeant Busbee introduced the other officers to Doug. Deputy Mike Alters was the mate on the boat and Deputy Sean Nelson was the diver.

Doug asked, "So Sean, tell me about your dive experience."

Sean answered, "Well, I got certified when I was 20. I've had about ten trips to the Keys, diving on the coral reefs down there, and thirty feet has been my deepest dive. I joined the Sheriff's Office two years ago, and we trained on some lakes. I've rescued two people from cars that ran off the road into a canal, and I retrieved the body of a jumper from the Ft. Myers Beach Bridge last summer."

Doug looked Sean over. He appeared to be in his late twenties, thin but athletic. He had no experience with deep dives, but appeared to be eager for the dive. Doug fondly remembered his youth when he had no fear. Doug explained the complexities of the Boca Grande pass current to Sean and how they would have to wear extra weights around their waist to reach the bottom. They would have heavy duty inflatable dive bags to collect any evidence, along with the normal dive gear.

Doug asked, "Any questions?"

Sean answered impatiently, "Yes. What exactly are we looking for?"

Doug understood Sean's frustration, "I'm not sure. Any wreckage from the boat that'd give us a clue to what happened. We'll try to reconstruct whatever evidence we find back on land."

Sean asked, "There's got to be a lot of man-made trash on the bottom. How will we know if it's from the *Two Tongues*?"

Doug answered, "All the other man-made items will have barnacles on them. It takes about a week for barnacles to form. Anything that doesn't have barnacles is from the *Two Tongues*."

Doug and Sean checked and rechecked their dive gear. Everything was ready, but Doug started to question whether the dive was really necessary when he remembered Sandy's bloody shoe on the bottom of his boat. Doug thought, by God, if anything is there, I'm going to find out what caused the explosion.

*   *   *   *   *

Sergeant Busbee slowed the boat as they approached the dive point. There was a steady breeze from the northwest that produced short waves, spaced close together. Divers use a tank with one hour of air attached to a life-buoy vest, known as a BC vest, around their neck. The BC vest inflates when a small handle is pulled and it has enough compressed air to float a man to the surface. They each had a double-sized belt of weights that would help take them to the bottom through the current.

The incoming tide had just reached the full point, and there would be a 20 to 30 minute slack tide before the tide would start rushing out. They each had a heavy-duty inflat-able dive bag to collect any evidence. Doug carried a bang stick, which was a shotgun shell loaded into an attachment on the end of a metal stick. If a shark got too close, he could press it against the skin and it would discharge. Sean carried a traditional spear gun, but Doug felt more secure with his bangstick.

Doug looked around the pass and said a silent prayer. Two Coast Guard boats kept the fishing fleet and the curi-ous boaters away from the dive area. Doug reminded Sean that when they returned to the surface they needed to allow enough air time because they'd have to go as slow as their bubbles, allowing their bodies to adjust to the pressure. If they didn't do this, they could get blockages in their arteries and veins, harming their internal organs.

Doug gave the thumbs up sign, jumped into the water, and Sean followed. Doug's eyes adjusted to the light and began swimming down. Suddenly, large silver shapes were all around them, and the school of tarpon scattered as they swam around the divers. Doug remembered it was strange that he didn't see any tarpon jumping in the pass, but he attributed it to the slack tide. Doug looked over at Sean and saw his eyes were as round as golf balls.

They continued their dive down into the dark, hazy blue water. After a minute of swimming, Doug saw the light, sandy bottom to his left, but there was only about 20 feet of visibility. On his right was the edge of the trench, and it was dark and uninviting. They swam down into the trench, turned on their flashlights, and looked around the jagged bottom. There was some bright coral and sponges on the limestone ledge, and lobsters stuck their head out of holes in the rocks. A five-foot pea-green moray eel swam from one rock to a bigger rock for more protection from the strange light. Doug looked back toward the surface and saw a light blue ceiling.

They spread out about twenty feet apart and started swimming with the prevailing current, looking for some clue. There were hundreds of broken fishing lines stuck on all the rocks. Lead jig heads were scattered across the bottom like leaves in the woods on a fall day. They had traveled about 200 yards when Doug saw something shiny behind a limestone ledge, and he signaled Sean and they swam toward it. Doug looked down at a long shiny pipe-like object.

He picked it up and realized it was the stainless steel shaft that turned the propeller. It was broken and only about

156

six feet long. He looked around and saw another shining object about five yards away, close to the wall of the trench. Doug dropped the shaft and swam over to the object. It was from the *Two Tongues* because it was bronze with no barnacles, but he didn't recognize the shape. He reached down and turned it over, disturbing the sand and momentarily creating a haze. He realized it was one of the rudders, unnaturally fused to a broken propeller. He looked at it closer and realized that the rudder had been forced into the propeller by the blast. The rudder had been forged, or somehow melted, together with the propeller.

Doug thought of the construction of the boat's propulsion system. There was at least eighteen inches between the rudder and the propeller. The force of the explosion from the engine room would've pushed them straight down, away from each other. For them to be bonded together by the explosion, the force had to come from behind the boat. Doug was confused. He didn't know the cause of the explosion, but he knew that this was a powerful piece of evidence.

Doug had just finished putting this evidence in the dive bag when the light from the sun was blocked by an eerie shadow. Doug looked up and saw a large hammerhead shark fifteen feet above him, biting down on a fleeing tarpon. The shark got the rear two-thirds of the tarpon. The bloody head portion drifted down and landed next to Sean. Doug looked at the large, abnormal amount of bubbles coming from Sean, and could tell he was panicking. Doug turned off his flash-light and let it fall to the ground.

He motioned for Sean to come closer, but he froze and dropped his flashlight on the ground, flashing an inviting light to the curious shark. Doug looked back up and saw the shark swimming above, looking for the remainder of the tarpon. The bloody tarpon piece was five feet from Sean, so Doug swam toward Sean and grabbed him, pulling him away from the bloody carcass. Doug looked back up and saw that Hitler was at least 25 feet long and swimming menacingly toward them.

Doug knew the spear gun wouldn't hurt Hitler, but he needed a diversion. He grabbed the spear gun from Sean and shot it at Hitler when he got about 15 feet away. It bounced off his side, but caused him to swim farther down the trench momentarily. Doug picked up the stainless steel shaft, grabbed Sean's hand, and pulled him to the wall of the trench. Doug looked to his right and saw a large shape coming at him. He instinctively held the shaft out in front of him, like a spear. The shape came into focus and he realized it was a goliath grouper the size of a Volkswagen. The goliath grouper looked at Doug and Sean and started a deep drum sound from its belly, a sound produced when a rival predator invades its territory.

Hitler raced in from above the top of the trench. He hovered over the bottom, turned on its side, and bit into the

158

bleeding tarpon head with his powerful jaws. Sean finally snapped out of it and held the stainless steel shaft as Doug pulled the dive bag, filled with the remains of the propeller and the rudder, in front of them. The grouper saw Hitler and slowly swam backwards until it was next to the wall of the trench, about ten feet from Doug. The grouper increased the volume of the drumbeat sound as Doug and Sean furiously tried to construct some type of protection with the shaft.

Hitler slowly swam toward Doug and Sean, so they huddled together, backed up against the trench wall, and both held the shaft in front of them like a spear. They had the rear of it wedged into the trench wall behind them. Doug was moving his feet around a rock to get a better grip on the shaft when his left arm hit a sharp piece of coral sticking out from the trench wall. He watched in disbelief as his blood flowed into the water from his wound.

Doug looked at Hitler's grapefruit-sized eyes as he inched closer to them. The black eye on each end of the grotesque head stared at them. There was about four feet of the stainless steel shaft between Hitler's teeth and their flesh. Doug looked over at Sean and saw the horror-stricken look of a trapped animal. Doug's arm was bleeding and he was running out of air while the goliath grouper continued his panicked drum sounds, which were deafening. In the confusion, Doug dropped his bang stick to the bottom of the trench. Hitler moved closer and rubbed the end of the shaft with his nose, testing the strength. Their situation was hope-less.

Doug decided he was not going to die in vain. He was going to get the dive bag, with the evidence, to the surface, no matter what happened to him. He pulled his mouthpiece and inserted it into the valve for the inflatable dive bag. The pressurized air quickly filled the dive bag and it floated toward the surface.

The sound and movement of the inflating dive bag startled the goliath grouper. He darted away from the edge of the trench wall and instinctively swam away from Hitler. The fleeing prey stimulated Hitler and with three strokes of his massive tail, he caught the goliath grouper and bit it in half. He swam slowly with the current, eating his large meal.

Doug pointed to the surface and they unfastened their weights, dropping them to the bottom. They started the swim to the surface, encouraged by their new lease on life. Halfway to the surface, Sean grabbed Doug and pointed to his air tank, signaling he was out of air. Doug took his mouthpiece out and gave it to Sean. Sean was still panick-ing and sucked the remaining air from Doug's tank. They unfastened their tanks, dropped them from their backs, and swam as fast as they could toward the surface. They didn't have time to follow their bubbles and allow the pressure in their body to adjust.

Doug was starting to get tunnel vision as he approached the surface. He could tell he was getting ready to pass out from lack of oxygen and the pressure in his head. He felt his arms getting heavy and the sunlight was dimming. He thought of Sandy's bloody shoe and got a boost of adrenaline and concentrated on swimming to the light. His lungs were almost ready to burst when he surfaced, gasped for air, and began treading water. The waves and outgoing tide pulled him toward the open Gulf as he looked around and saw Sean flailing his arms at the small Coast Guard inflatable boat racing towards them. They had made it.

Chapter 21

The Coast Guard inflatable boat picked Doug and Sean out of the water. Sean was hyperventilating and yelling incoherently about sharks and being bitten in half. Doug was concentrating on breathing and saying a silent prayer in thanks. When he looked over the side of the inflatable boat, he thought he saw a large shadow. The small Coast Guard boat transported them to the Coast Guard cutter, *Pointe Steel*, for medical treatment. Both Doug and Sean were given oxygen masks, and after ten minutes of breathing pure oxygen, their breathing was back to normal. Sean was no longer talking; he just stared straight ahead. Sergeant Busbee had tied up the Sheriff's boat to the *Pointe Steel* and came aboard to find out what had happened.

The Coast Guard Captain, Scott Blain, had assembled everyone in the galley to talk about the dive. Doug told the group what had happened in the trench and everyone was speechless and secretly thanked God they weren't with them on the bottom. Sean just looked at the group with a blank stare and said nothing. Captain Blain told Doug the inflatable boat had recovered the dive bag and it was on the top deck of the *Pointe Steel*. Doug asked them to bring the dive bag into the galley so they could all examine the evidence.

Sergeant Busbee was concerned about Sean. He was still not responding to questions and his pupils were dilated. Captain Blain suggested he might be in shock, prompting Sergeant Busbee to call for an air ambulance on his portable radio to meet him at the Boca Grande lighthouse beach. Sean was taken to the Sheriff's boat and Sergeant Busbee told Doug he would be back after the air ambulance picked up Sean.

The Coast Guard First Mate brought the dive bag into the galley and emptied it on the floor. Doug and Captain Blain examined the twisted wreckage as Doug talked about the rest of his investigation. The First Mate brought them fresh hot coffee as they pondered the brass and bronze wreckage at their feet. It looked like an industrial strength trash compactor had attempted to crush them and they had melted together into a contorted mass.

Captain Blain finally spoke after a few minutes of silent thought, "A bomb. A bomb planted on the rear of the boat would produce a force that'd explain the wreckage. This rudder and propeller wreckage looks like some of the pictures from Vietnam blasts. Those bastards were good with bombs."

Doug was stunned, but yet it made sense. He asked, "But why? Why would someone want to kill Sandy?"

164

Captain Blain cocked his head to the left and asked, "Who else was on the boat?"

Doug conceded he'd been more concerned about his dead friend than properly investigating the accident with the other victims' histories in mind. Doug realized that this was now a murder investigation. He had a lot of work to do before the trail of the killer got cold. Someone had killed Doug's best friend in front of him and thought he could get away with it. It was possible that Sandy was not the target, but merely collateral damage, which energized him more with anger.

Captain Blain and Doug exchanged their theories on what type of bomb and detonator were used. They both agreed it would take a professional to secure a bomb to a boat that moved at fast speeds. Doug knew it was a large amount of quality explosives that caused such a devastating inferno.

Sergeant Busbee returned to the *Pointe Steel* to pick up Doug and the evidence. As he guided the boat back to Pineland Marina, Doug told him Captain Blain's theory about a bomb, and Sergeant Busbee agreed that it made sense. Doug used his cell phone to call Miller's Marina, got the name of Sandy's charters that day and their credit card numbers. Doug turned to Sergeant Busbee and said, "His charter for the whole week were two doctors out of Atlanta. A Dr. Chadwick "Chad" Elsworth III, and Dr. Charles "Trip"

Cleland III were aboard with Sandy and Miguel when the *Two Tongues* exploded. I'm gonna call the computer geeks at the Department and have 'em run their names through the national data banks."

The national data banks were put together by the FBI. With a credit card number, they access your Social Security Number, all loans and other credit cards with the outstanding balances, all bank accounts and stock accounts with the balances. They can access the tax rolls of every state and find out if you own real estate there. They can access the court filings of every state to find out every past or currently pending lawsuit. They also check your criminal history in every state. Doug called his favorite investigator in the Sheriff's computer department, Todd Holberg, and told him to process his requested search on the two doctors ASAP. Doug instructed Todd to e-mail the results to his home computer as soon as he had the report.

Once at Pineland Marina, Doug loaded the wreckage into his truck. He drove back to his house without the radio on while deep in thought about the events of the past two days. His thoughts became muddled and he was starting to develop a headache as he pulled into his driveway. He was sweaty, tired, and hungry as he unloaded the wreckage into his garage.

It felt good to get inside his air-conditioned house, and he opened his refrigerator and looked for something to eat.

There was very little food to choose from, so he finally de-cided on two-day old leftover pizza, still in the delivery box, which he ate cold and washed down with a glass of tea. He suddenly felt exhausted, walked into his bedroom, lay down on his bed without taking off his clothes or pulling the covers back, and instantly fell into a deep sleep.

Chapter 22

Doug woke from his afternoon nap at four in the morning. He was refreshed and his mind clear. He hurried over to his computer and turned it on. The e-mail box showed he had mail from the Sheriff's Office, and he punched in his password to retrieve the report on the Atlanta doctors. Dr. Charles "Trip" Cleland III had no loans, lawsuits, arrests, or outstanding warrants. He owned a house valued at $220,000, with a $100,000 mortgage in Atlanta. He was single and had a stock portfolio worth $80,000. There was nothing noteworthy from this preliminary report.

Dr. Chadwick "Chad" Elsworth III had a more interesting report. He had over $85,000 in cash advances on his credit cards in the past 30 days. His wife had filed for divorce, and he had been sued for malpractice in the past 30 days. He had a business checking account with a $462 balance, and he had no savings account or stock portfolio. He and his wife owned a house in Atlanta worth $425,000, a first mortgage of $300,000 and a second mortgage of $150,000. Dr. Elsworth had also been arrested for domestic violence the week before. His wife certainly didn't grieve when the good doctor died. Doug's detective instincts made him wonder how much life insurance there was for Dr. Elsworth.

Drs. Elsworth and Cleland had flown into Ft. Myers that Tuesday. They were staying at Cabbage Key and Sandy had picked them up Wednesday and fished. Sandy had picked them up Thursday and was getting ready to fish when they all were blown up. Doug felt nauseous and decided to walk into his backyard for a breath of fresh air. He walked down to his seawall to look under his dock lights for any fish. Doug was looking at a school of baitfish swimming in the light when he heard female laughter and giggles to his left, over at his neighbor's pool.

His neighbors were a retired couple that lived down south in the winter and back in Ohio during the summer. He remembered that the neighbor's granddaughter and her girlfriend had arrived two days ago for a vacation in the vacant house. The two girls were young and pretty and had apparently met a couple of the local boys. Doug stood and watched as the skinny-dipping foursome enjoyed themselves, until he felt like a peeping Tom. As he walked back to his house, he couldn't help feeling old.

He ate a quick breakfast and showered. He went out to his garage to look at the wreckage. If it was a bomb, someone had to place it on the boat undetected. At Miller's Marina a stranger would stand out, so he decided to go to Cabbage Key to see his old friend, Rob Wells, and ask the employees if they had seen anything unusual. Doug made sure he closed his back door very loudly. He walked down to his dock, faking loud coughs to alert his frisky neighbors. The pool was empty. Apparently, they had retired to the confines of the house for the remainder of their youthful, nocturnal games.

As he eased his boat down the quiet canal, the sun was starting to rise over the mangrove jungle on the east side of the Matlacha River. It was low tide, so he had to stay in the marked channel. The no-see-ums were buzzing in his nose and ears until he powered his boat up on plane and headed north around Pine Island to Cabbage Key. A flock of pelicans were flying in formation over the calm water of the Matlacha River. Doug followed them until they turned east toward the mainland.

At 7:00 a.m. he was docking at Cabbage Key. He walked up the shell mound to the restaurant, walked in and saw Rob sitting at a table, eating breakfast and reading the newspaper. Doug walked over to him and asked, "Hey, how are the pancakes?"

Rob looked up over his paper and looked surprised. "How're you doing, Doug? It was terrible what happened to Sandy."

The waitress brought a cup of coffee to Doug, and Rob asked him to sit down at his table. Doug explained to Rob what he saw in the pass and what evidence they had found.

He explained the Coast Guard Captain's theory about the bomb, and Rob sat in silence processing all of the information. The screen door to the restaurant opened and Rob's wife, Phyllis, walked in wearing jogging gear. She joined them, and the waitress brought her orange juice and water. Doug repeated his story to Phyllis.

Doug said, "I came out here to ask you and your employees if they saw anything, or anyone, unusual on the morning the *Two Tongues* blew up."

Phyllis answered, "Well, now that you bring it up, I did see something different the morning of the explosion. I was finishing my morning jog around the island and coming up the west trail. I saw a man with snorkeling gear getting into his boat at the dock. I remember wondering what he was doing, but I didn't think anything of it. I figured he dropped something overboard."

Doug stared in amazement as he realized he had found his smoking gun. He stammered, "What kind of boat was it? What did he look like?"

Phyllis said, "Well, he was probably a hundred yards away. I couldn't see his face too well, but he had dark hair and a thin, muscular build. He was in one of those small rental boats from Jenson's Marina."

Rob asked the waitress to wake up Nate. A few minutes later, Nate stumbled into the dining room with his hair disheveled. Doug repeated the story and Phyllis described

172

the man.

Nate shook his head slowly and said, "Yeah, I remember him. He checked in on Wednesday afternoon. He drank Evian water and ice, and was asking about chartering a fishing boat. Wednesday night around eight, he came out from his room and said he wanted to leave early the next morning, so he paid his tab."

Doug asked excitedly, "Do you have a copy of his credit card?"

Nate shook his head. "No, he paid in cash. Nice tipper."

Doug finished his coffee and thanked Phyllis for her help. He left Cabbage Key and headed south to Jenson's Marina as fast as his boat would run. His 10-year-old Johnson engine was starting to show its age as it struggled at high speeds. He made a mental note to start calling around for engine prices. After a twenty-minute ride, he slowed down off plane as he approached Jenson's dock. People in other boats glared at him because he was ignoring the no-wake zone. Doug docked his boat at Jenson's Marina, jumped off, and ran down the long pier to the office.

Doug had to catch his breath as he entered the rental office. Doug explained to the manager he was a detective with the Sheriff's office and he was conducting a murder investigation. Doug asked about the process for renting a boat, and the manager said a driver's license is required. Doug described the visitor from Cabbage Key and asked if they kept a copy of his driver's license. The manager nodded and pulled the rental file, and found a copy of the visitor's driver's license.

The picture was that of a hispanic male, and the name and address on the license were for a Frank Ortiz, 233 Third Street, Miami, FL. The manager gave a copy of the driver's license to Doug. The manager confirmed that the renter looked like the photograph on the driver's license. Doug put it in a plastic bag to keep it dry, thanked the manager, and ran back to his boat. The adrenaline was flowing, and Doug was ready to find the killer of his best friend. He wasn't certain whether he would arrest the man or dispense his own brand of justice. Doug ran his boat at top speed back to his house. He doubted that the name or address was correct, but he had a good picture. He called the Miami police and told them he needed a murder suspect picked up for questioning.

Doug called Todd Holberg at the Sheriff's computer division and told him he was going to scan a copy of a driver's license into his computer and e-mail it to him. After he received it, he needed him to run this ASAP through the FBI's computer to get a correct name and address. An hour later, Doug got a call back from the Miami Police, who told him that the address listed didn't exist. He wasn't surprised; a professional hit man would have dozens of false identifications.

Doug got a quick shower and fixed a sandwich. The

light on his computer started blinking, signaling an e-mail. He quickly typed his password into the computer. The e-mail was from the FBI, giving the name of the person on the picture as Carlos Rodriquez, aka "Iceman," address unknown. He was known to stay in the Miami area and was a suspect in numerous murders, but no convictions. He was dishonorably discharged from the Army, where he had been a Ranger. Doug had his man—now just needed to find him.

Chapter 23

Doug called Mark Simion, one of his friends from the Drug Enforcement Agency. Mark had been with the DEA for 15 years and worked all over South Florida putting drug dealers in prison. He worked in Ft. Myers as an undercover agent and Doug had assisted him in a number of drug raids.

Mark answered the phone, "Hi there, Doug. What's cooking?" Doug explained everything that had happened in the past three days and his problem with Carlos.

Doug said, "I want this guy bad. He killed my best friend, Sandy. I was hopin' to call in a big favor. I want to drive with you to Miami and meet with your people over there. I want to show Carlos' picture to all of your drug dealer defendants awaiting sentencing to see if they know where he's staying. If they give us a good address and we make an arrest, they can get their sentence cut by cooperating with law enforcement. What do you think?"

Mark agreed it was a big favor. However, Doug had helped him in the past. Mark had been a target of an internal investigation involving excessive force on an arrested drug dealer. Mark had seen the drug dealer shoot and kill his friend and fellow officer in a botched drug raid in Ft. Myers. Doug and two other members of the Sheriff's Department were assisting DEA when they attempted to serve a search warrant at a drug dealer's house. There were five suspects with automatic weapons and a bloody gun battle broke out when they entered the residence. One officer was killed and three wounded, but four of the suspects were killed. The one remaining living suspect was arrested by Mark and endured a beating in the back bedroom. Doug had been shot in the chest but was fortunately wearing a bulletproof vest. He'd killed two of the suspects himself and also wanted revenge. But he was able to hold back as he watched Mark pistol-whip the suspect. Doug was the only other witness and had backed up Mark's false story of self-defense. After the internal investigation was over, Mark told Doug privately that if he ever needed anything, he was there for him.

Mark said, "Let's do it. Be here at three this afternoon, and we'll drive over. We'll go to Little Havana and have a nice dinner."

Doug quickly packed. When he checked his answering machine, there were 12 messages on it from Sandy's family regarding the burial and asking Doug to be a pallbearer. He called and told them he couldn't because of the investigation. Sandy's father, Big Papa, became angry when he said he couldn't give out details because it was an ongoing investigation. The harsh words from Big Papa hurt, but there was no other way. He would pay his respects to Sandy after he caught his killer.

Doug arrived at the DEA office and loaded his gear into Mark's sedan at 3:00 p.m. On the trip over to Miami, Doug drove and Mark was on his cell phone lining up interviews with drug dealer defendants for the following morning. By the time they arrived in Miami, 14 defendants had been scheduled for interviews the next morning at the local DEA office. All of his potential informants were repeat drug dealers with significant criminal histories. They were also the types of people to hire Carlos to eliminate some of their competition.

Doug and Mark arrived in Miami at sunset, checked into their motel and unpacked. They went to Little Havana for some Cuban food and music. After a large dinner, they had spiced rum with their cigars, and Doug talked about escaping from Hitler. Mark didn't believe Hitler's size, but refused an offer to go diving with Doug so they could measure him. They returned to their hotel room and slept soundly.

The next morning they didn't get a positive response until their last interview. The drug dealer, Martine Lunez, got really nervous. He told them that "Iceman" was feared in the Miami underworld because of his methods and his desire for absolute privacy. He heard Iceman moved every few months. However, he had delivered a bag of money, at his supplier's request, to him at a condo on Miami Beach three weeks ago. Doug showed him the picture from Carlos's false driver's license, and he confirmed it was the same person.

Doug and Mark took Martine Lunez on a ride to Miami Beach. He was very reluctant to show them Carlos' condo because he feared for his family. Carlos had a reputation in the Hispanic community of killing children of people he felt dishonored him. After promises of less prison time, he reluctantly showed them the condo on the east wing of a 20-story beachfront building.

Doug and Mark quickly returned to the DEA office, where Doug asked to use a computer. He typed an affidavit, describing the evidence of the murders and how he had arrived in Miami to confirm the murder suspect's residence. He then faxed the affidavit to the Lee County Sheriff's Office. Doug had one of his fellow detectives fill out the paperwork for a search warrant of the condo in Miami Beach. The detective took it to the Lee County courthouse for a circuit judge's signature on the search warrant. Two hours later, Doug and Mark received the signed search warrant by fax. They called for the Miami police to assist them in serving the warrant.

Doug, Mark, and four members of the Miami Police Department approached the condo, where they knocked and announced their presence. When there was no answer, they busted down the door with a battering ram and entered with their guns drawn. No one was there. There were some clothes in the closet and a little food in the refrigerator. There were no guns or explosives, only a computer on the dining room table. There was no other evidence in the sparsely furnished condo.

They seized the computer pursuant to the search warrant. No other item had any evidentiary value. Doug was angry with himself; he should have staked out the condo and verified that Carlos was home before they raided his apartment. The Miami Police put out an all points bulletin for Carlos. Doug knew it was too late; Carlos would go underground and be virtually impossible to find.

Carlos had a beeper that he kept with him at all times. The alarm system on his condo was rigged to dial 911 on his beeper if his apartment door was opened. Carlos had paid the condo maintenance man to be a lookout for him. When his beeper went off, he called the cell phone of the maintenance man who told him the police were searching his apartment. Carlos thanked the maintenance man and turned the power off on his phone. He threw it into a trash dumpster in case the police knew his number and were triangulating his location with the phone company's sending antennas.

Carlos had planned for this contingency. He abandoned his car at a grocery store and hailed a cab. He went to one of his frequent employers, who was also a friend, who arranged for Carlos to hide on a freighter carrying supplies to Colombia that was leaving that night. Carlos went to his rented storage unit and grabbed a suitcase he kept for emergencies that was full of cash and false identifications.

Before he left for the Port of Miami, he called his bank in Switzerland and had his entire savings of four million dollars transferred to a numbered account he had in Colombia's National Bank. He knew he could never return to the United States and he didn't care. He could live very well in Colombia on his money.

Chapter 24

Doug and Mark drove back to Ft. Myers that night with the seized computer in the back seat. Doug told Mark the summary of the data bank search for the two doctors. They both agreed that Dr. Elsworth was the probable target, and money and love are the two most common motives. Doug planned his next step of the investigation. He was still angry that he didn't stake out Carlos' condo and swore to himself he would be more patient when he had a lead next time.

Mark dropped Doug off at the DEA building at 10:00 p.m. and transferred the computer to his truck. He drove to the Lee County Sheriff's Office and left the computer to be analyzed by their experts, with a note to call him at home as soon as they had finished. He went by his desk, and there were over 50 messages about different investigations. There was a message from Sean Nelson thanking him for helping him on the dive and that he was taking a week's vacation to relax in the mountains, away from water.

Doug drove home listening to the country music, and he thought how over the years his taste in music had gradually changed from rock to country. After the past four days, he longed for a normal life with a wife, kids, and a loyal dog. It had been five months since Doug broke up with his last girlfriend. It would be nice to lay down on his couch with his head in her lap while she gently massaged his head and he talked about what a bad day he had. He snapped out of his fantasy as he slowed to drive across the Matlacha Bridge. One of the bridge fishermen had just pulled a big snapper over the rail and was trying to unhook it.

The moon was shining brightly as Doug drove into his driveway. He unpacked and looked in his refrigerator for something to eat. He settled on a cheese sandwich and some potato chips and grabbed a cold beer to wash it down. After he finished his late dinner, he decided to have another beer. The beer had tasted exceptionally good after being in the outdoor humidity. He turned on his TV, watched the news, and within five minutes became depressed with all the bad news, and turned off the TV.

He went to the refrigerator and got a third beer. He was enjoying the high and the relaxation from the beer when he decided to go outside to look for fish around his dock. As he was enjoying the bright moonlight, he heard the familiar female laughs and giggles from next door. He suddenly felt very depressed and went back inside.

Doug walked to his sink and poured out his half-empty beer and decided to take a shower to relax. As he stepped into his shower, he stubbed his toe on his drain. The old brass drain had been bent upward since he bought his house seven years ago. Over the years, he had gotten into the habit of stepping into the shower on one side and avoiding the drain. He had developed a weird ritual while he showered of standing on one foot to avoid the bent drain while washing his left side and then reversing his footing when washing his right side.

The ritual normally kept him from stubbing his toe. On days, such as today, when he was preoccupied he would forget and hit his toe. Today was different—he was angry and it was time to fix the damn drain. He put on shorts, pulled the drain up and went to his garage. He put the bent drain in his vise, grabbed a pair of pliers, and bent the drain so it was even. The entire process took less than three minutes. He took the drain back to the shower and replaced it. He stripped and stepped into the middle of his shower, on top of the drain, and it was such a great feeling. For seven years he had gotten into the habit of avoiding the broken drain instead of fixing it. He wondered how many other habits he had developed over the years to compensate for something that could be fixed easily.

Doug dried off, walked into his living room and turned on his stereo. The country music relaxed him as he sat in his recliner and thought of Sandy. He felt tears forming on the corner of his eyes. He tried to stop them, but he couldn't. He cried uncontrollably until there were no tears left and then fell asleep in his recliner, with the country music providing a background for his lonely dreams.

He woke up to the phone ringing. It was Todd Holberg from the computer department of the Sheriff's office with news of nothing exceptional in the computer. It had been hooked up to the Internet, and Carlos had downloaded a few joke pages into the computer memory and a few nude photographs of celebrities. Doug said he would be by later and pick up the computer.

Doug was back to square one. He pulled out the report on Dr. Chadwick Elsworth and looked for the name of the lawyer on the opposite side of the malpractice lawsuit. Even though it was Saturday morning, Doug called Karen Senard's office. After telling the answering service it was a police emergency, they put his call through. Karen picked up the phone and identified herself. Doug told Karen how he got her name and why he thought the explosion was a planned murder. He then asked whether there was anything unusual about the lawsuit with Dr. Elsworth.

Karen said, "Dr. Elsworth had brought the HMO insurance company into the lawsuit as a third-party defendant, alleging they were illegally denying valid claims for MRIs."

Doug said, "Wait a minute, ma'am. Could you explain that to me in English."

Karen gave Doug the background and the problem with no malpractice insurance. Doug was beginning to understand the reasoning behind the third-party lawsuit, and it sounded like a good murder motive to him.

Karen said, "Guess what? On top of all that, the law firm that represents LAMPCO has hired Dr. Elsworth's lawyer as a partner. He's filed a motion to withdraw as counsel for Dr. Elsworth, claiming it's a conflict of interest, and he won't even take my phone calls. Before Dr. Elsworth's death, he was begging me to meet with him, so he could tell me some dirt on LAMPCO."

Doug was getting excited with his new lead. Karen and Doug traded details about their different, but connected cases. Suddenly, Karen thought of a way to prove a connection between LAMPCO and Carlos.

Karen asked, "Do you still have Carlos' computer?"

Doug said, "Yes, but our investigators couldn't find anything."

Karen said, "I have a paralegal who's a computer whiz. We've gotten access to hospitals' computers and pulled hidden, deleted information from the computer's memory. We could fly down today and look at the computer. She might be able to find something in the computer's memory that your people overlooked. She really is quite talented with computers."

Doug said, "That'd be great. You could bring your information on LAMPCO, and I could run it through our national data banks to check on them. We could share information, and it'd help both of us."

Karen said, "You got a deal. Give me your number and I'll call back with the flight information."

As he gave Karen his number, he couldn't help wondering if she was as good looking as her voice sounded.

Chapter 25

Doug met Karen and Jamie at the Delta Terminal in the Ft. Myers airport. Karen was wearing loose-fitting khaki pants and a tight canary yellow polo shirt with penny loafers. Her hair was pulled back in a ponytail that made her look athletic and adventurous. As she walked toward Doug, he could tell how extremely cold she was. He caught himself admiring the view and forced himself to focus on Karen's face.

After polite introductions, Karen said, "That was the most gorgeous approach over the beach before we landed. Do you live near the beach?"

Doug replied, "I don't live near the beach, but I live on a canal. The beach is about a 30 minute ride in my boat."

Jamie asked, "I heard that Floridians don't go to the beach much. When was the last time you went?"

Doug replied, "I'm in the sun when I'm fishing, but I bet it's been 10 years since I went to the beach."

They laughed as they headed toward the escalator. Doug was embarrassed when Jamie asked where the elevator was. They walked next to Jamie as she rolled her wheelchair toward the elevator across the reception area. As they approached Doug's truck, he debated about where Jamie would sit. His truck was not exactly made for wheelchairs, but Jamie was a sport about it. She told Doug the wheelchair was just a ploy so she could have men pick her up and put her in their trucks. Doug secured Jamie's wheelchair in the back of his truck after lifting her into the seat.

Doug had always driven Ford trucks with the Firestone tires. Doug's dad had worked as a gardener for Ford's and Firestone's estates, next to the Edison home in downtown Ft. Myers, when he was a teenager. Doug's dad had met both of the men and liked them. He thought locals should drive Fords with Firestone tires to show their respect, so that's all he ever drove.

In the truck, Karen sat in the middle, next to Doug. Her perfume was extremely stimulating to Doug, especially when he noticed there was no ring on her left hand. He hadn't dated for the past five months, and it'd been even longer since he was this attracted to a woman. She had beauty and brains—there had to be a catch, he thought to himself.

Jamie asked, "What type of computer is it?"

Doug said, "It's a Dell computer with a rebuilt Compaq monitor. Our computer experts couldn't find much."

Jamie replied confidently, "I'm sure I'll find something. What's the bet?"

Doug laughed and said, "A seafood dinner."

Jamie said, "You got it. Start counting your money."

Karen had been pleasantly surprised when she saw Doug. He didn't have the standard doughnut belly of middle-age cops. Karen was impressed when Doug easily lifted Jamie up in the truck. Karen had caught a glimpse of the back of his jeans while loading their luggage in the truck bed; the rear looked as good as the front.

Karen always looked at men's eyes as a gauge of their personality. It was a litmus test to whether she would date a man. She agreed with the famous writer that eyes are the windows to a man's soul. She thought Doug's green eyes showed kindness and strength. They left the airport and drove to the Sheriff's Office, picked up the computer, and secured it in the back. As they drove to Matlacha, Doug fascinated them with the details of his encounter with Hitler.

It was dinnertime by the time they reached Doug's house. He unloaded the computer, set it up on the dining room table, and Jamie immediately started to work. He asked if they wanted fresh fish for dinner. They were both impressed and said yes. Doug grabbed a fishing rod with an artificial lure and went out back to catch dinner. Karen excused herself and went to freshen up.

When she returned, Jamie asked, "I saw how you were lookin' at him. Are you going to mix business with pleasure?"

Karen blushed and said, "I don't know, maybe. He is

191

kinda cute. When I went to the bathroom, I looked in his closets and didn't see any evidence of a female living here."

Jamie feigned shock and said, "You just met this man and you're snooping through his things. I know it's been a while for you, but have some dignity."

Karen went to the refrigerator and grabbed three beers. After looking in his sparse refrigerator, Karen was certain Doug was a determined bachelor. Karen opened a beer for Jamie and set it next to the computer. She opened the other two and went outside. Doug had already caught two trout and was bringing in a third, when Karen walked out with the beer. He took the trout off his lure and threw it on the ground, next to the others. Karen handed him the open beer, and he took a long drink and sat it down on his cleaning table.

He picked up a trout and his filet knife and asked, "Have you ever eaten seatrout before?"

Karen answered, "No, but I had some mountain trout when I was vacationing up in Blowing Rock, North Carolina."

Doug started cleaning the moving fish on a table bolted to his dock and said, "I bet you never had fish this fresh before."

Karen said, "No, but I can't wait."

Karen watched in amazement as a dozen pelicans flew up and landed on the dock next to them. Doug threw the

192

scraps in the air and watched them fight. In the rear of the group of pelicans was an old gray one with some monofilament fishing line wrapped around a wing. Doug saw how he walked with a limp and made sure he threw a couple of pieces over the others to him.

When Doug brought the fresh trout fillets into his kitchen, Jamie was impressed that he caught and cleaned dinner so fast. She continued to work on Carlos' computer while Karen sat at the breakfast bar, drinking beer and watching this intriguing, rugged-looking cop fix her dinner of fried trout and pasta. Karen enjoyed the warm feeling that came over her, and she had to cross and re-cross her legs three times while Doug fixed dinner. It'd been a long time since a man had caused her body to react like that.

After dinner was ready, Jamie took a break from the computer and they all enjoyed the fresh trout. The women quickly cleaned their plates and refilled them, clearly enjoying the incredible dinner. After dinner, Jamie returned to the computer, and Karen watched in amazement as Doug cleaned up the kitchen without asking for her help. His house was clean and he was a good cook. There was only one more requirement and he would be the perfect man.

Karen and Doug grabbed some fresh beer and went outside to watch the sunset. As they sat down on the seawall, Karen asked, "How did you get that scar?"

Doug replied, "When Sandy and I were in college, we

went to a redneck bar and got into a scrap. I didn't know I was talking to the ex-wife of a jealous and violent man. He and his friends jumped me when Sandy went to the bathroom. I was getting my ass kicked and then they broke a beer bottle on my face. I thought I was gonna die. Sandy ran out to his truck and got a shotgun with one shell. He fired it to get everybody's attention and then bluffed his way out with me. He saved my life, and I was lucky that I only have this one scar."

Karen asked, "What was he like?"

Doug replied, "He was the life of the party. He always had a good joke and a funny story to tell. All of the women loved him. I remember this attractive snowbird from New Jersey that spent every winter at Boca Grande. She always had a thing for Sandy, but when she got divorced, she chased him shamelessly. She ordered a dozen red roses to be sent to Miller's Marina so they'd be waiting for him when he finished his charter. The snowbird didn't know that Sandy used to date the lady who owned the florist shop. She was mad and changed the note that went with the flowers to:

I'm glad your test results are negative. I swear I didn't know I had anything.

Love, Sharon.

"The florist lady delivered the flowers to Miller's Marina. However, the florist lady didn't know the lady that ran the ship's store also used to date Sandy. She read the note and went ballistic. When Sandy came in that day, she grabbed the roses and threw them at Sandy in front of his charter and all of the other guides at the dock."

Karen said, "He sounds like he was a good friend to have."

As a tear ran down his cheek, Doug replied, "The best."

They sat in silence and watched the sun set. A family of dolphins chased a school of mullet into the canal. When the dolphins forced them to the end of the canal, the feeding frenzy started. Dolphins charged into the middle of the trapped school and grabbed dinner. Many of the mullet jumped in the air to avoid being eaten. One of the dolphins jumped out of the water and caught one in midair. After the feeding frenzy was over Doug said, "It's time for another beer."

As he opened the back door for her, their eyes locked, just as Jamie yelled, "Yes, I've got the scumbags."

Doug asked, "What is it?"

Jamie proudly explained, "I accessed the hard drive on the computer and went through all of his old deleted messages on his e-mail and the addresses he accessed on the Internet for the past month. I found two very interesting things. The first thing is that I found a message from Al Brognese, the senior vice president of LAMPCO, to Carlos. The message was, "The money has been transferred." Minutes after this e-mail, Carlos accessed a Swiss bank on their website. I don't know the message or directions to the bank because Carlos communicated with numbers directly to the bank's Internet program."

Doug was amazed and said, "That's great. We now have a direct connection between Carlos and LAMPCO. I'll call the State Attorney's Office on Monday and find out if we need anything else before we make an arrest. It's time to celebrate—we solved the case!

"I have a toast I'd like to make. Sandy's favorite toast was, 'To living as long as you want, and wanting as long as you live.' Let's drink to that."

They clinked their beer cans and all took a drink. Karen walked next to Doug, put her hand heavily on his back and said, "I really like that toast. Is there a bar nearby? I want something stronger than beer, maybe a tequila shot."

Doug thought for a second and suggested, "Let's go to Cabbage Key. That's the perfect place to celebrate solving this case."

Jamie could see she was going to be a third wheel and declined, saying she was tired. Besides, she thought, Karen is always easier to work with when she has a man.

* * * * *

When Jamie finished rehabilitation after her airplane crash, she noticed that her legs had shrunk. The muscles had shrunk from lack of use, and her legs were bony. Her skin grew milky white because of the lack of sun and proper blood circulation. Before the accident, Jamie had a well-toned body from her long distance running and golf. It was depressing for her to watch her body deteriorate.

She decided that the portion of her body that could still move would stay in top shape. She developed an exercise program that she followed every morning. She positioned her legs on a coffee table and put two chairs even with her shoulders. She put each hand on a chair and did dips between the chairs. After that she would lie on the floor and slowly pull the coffee table over and set it on her legs. She needed this leverage so she could do her sit-ups. After her abdominal exercises, she used barbells for curls. Her morning exercises took an hour, but it was the best part of her day.

Jamie had two wheelchairs. Her normal wheelchair was made for both inside and outside use. It had wide rubber wheels with an optional power unit. When she had short distances to travel she pushed with her arms. When she had longer distances to travel she used the battery-powered switch. The toggle control was by her right hand mounted on the inside armrest.

The second wheelchair was used when she went shopping or some activity she needed to carry something. It had a basket in the back and narrower rubber wheels. It had a double battery pack and could go faster. The neighborhood kids loved it when she would race them on their tricycles. Jamie enjoyed watching them laugh and play. She also wanted to teach them to be comfortable around people in wheelchairs.

*   *   *   *   *

Doug and Karen got in Doug's boat and slowly headed out to the channel with the full moon rising on the horizon. There was no wind, so the reflection of the moon on the calm water was perfect. Doug powered his boat up on plane and headed north around Pine Island and then headed west to Cabbage Key. The moon was so bright they didn't need a spotlight to see the channel markers.

Karen was thoroughly relaxed. She helped solve a murder, and it should help her settle her civil case for big bucks. She met and connected with a handsome and interesting man. She was now in a boat, gliding across the water with the glow of the full moon showing the way. They were going to an island resort to drink, dance, and romance. Karen felt better than she had in decades.

They laughed and told jokes on the way to Cabbage Key. As they were docking at Cabbage Key, Doug asked, "What do you get when you cross a lawyer with a goat?

Karen smiled and said, "I don't know."

Doug replied, "Nothing. There are some things a goat just won't do."

She started giggling and then laughing uncontrollably. Doug smiled because the giggling and laughter reminded him of the young girls next door when they were skinny-dipping with their new boyfriends. All of sudden, he didn't feel so old.

They walked up the shell mound to the bar. As the door opened, they could hear the guitar player singing James Taylor's song, "*Sweet Baby James,*" and Karen started laughing. When Doug asked what was so funny about the song, Karen just smiled and said it was one of her favorite songs in college. She ordered a bottle of Chablis and tequila shots for both of them.

There were about twenty other people at the bar. Some of the people sang along with their favorite songs and entertained the others. A few couples danced between the tables oblivious to the others. Two couples in the back of the bar were playing Sexual Trivial Pursuit. Doug surmised with the constant orders of cocktails and their loud laughter, it would be a high scoring game.

They enjoyed the music and the wine until midnight when they decided to leave. They walked down the shell mound, hand in hand, and slowly down the dock to Doug's boat. They looked up at the full moon, now shining directly above them. The glow of the moon and shadows of the islands were incredibly sensual. As they slowly moved together, their first kiss was electric.

They left Cabbage Key and headed back to Matlacha, holding onto each other. When they entered the Matlacha River, Karen reached over and pulled the throttle back, slowing the boat off plane.

Doug asked, "What's the matter?"

Karen answered quietly, "Nothing. I was hoping we could anchor and watch the stars."

Doug slowed the boat, steered clear of the channel, turned the engine off, and threw out the anchor. After Doug secured the anchor, he turned around and Karen grabbed his arm, gently pulling him down onto the deck. Minutes turned into hours and the hours passed by quickly. By the time Karen and Doug looked up at the stars, the sun was rising.

Chapter 26

Doug pulled his boat up to his dock as the sun burnt off the morning dew. As he helped Karen out of the boat, he heard giggling and laughter. He looked over to his neighbor's house and saw the granddaughter and her friend on the patio having breakfast. He waved at them and smiled. He realized he felt a lot younger than when he last saw them.

When Doug and Karen walked in the back door, Jamie was watching TV. Jamie said, "You kids were out past curfew. You're grounded for a week."

Doug and Karen smiled and mumbled something about the boat breaking down. They both ate a light breakfast and then went to Doug's bedroom for some sleep. Karen's plane was scheduled to leave at four p.m., so they set the alarm for one and fell into a deep, relaxed sleep. The alarm woke up Karen, but Doug slept right through it. She smiled and turned the alarm off, got up and went to the kitchen for some juice. Jamie was outside on the porch looking at the canal. Karen showered, got dressed, and woke up Doug with a kiss. He rolled over and smiled as they made plans for Karen to fly down the following weekend. Doug looked at the clock, got up and showered.

He drove them to the airport, arriving at three. The sun and humidity was draining as he carried their luggage to the terminal and stayed with them until boarding. He couldn't believe how fast he had fallen for Karen, and she was enjoying the attention. After Doug gave Karen a long goodbye kiss, Karen and Jamie boarded the plane to Atlanta.

Once they settled in their seats, Jamie said, "I want the details; don't hold back."

Karen laughed and said, "Well, we went to Cabbage Key, had a few drinks, and listened to music. On the way back we ran up on a sandbar and had to wait on high tide."

Jamie said, "Yeah, right. I'm sure there was something rising, but it wasn't the tide. I can't believe you're going out with a cop. He's going to tell all his friends that he's dating a law tart. Remember the Georgia State Trooper that you dated? He wanted you to quit your job and raise his children from his first marriage."

Karen said, "No, he's not like that; he's very independent. He would want me to keep practicing law. He's also a gentleman; he won't kiss and tell."

Jamie rolled her eyes and said, "Whatever you say, boss. He must have a mole in the right place."

An hour later they were in a holding pattern over Atlanta. They circled for 30 minutes before they were allowed to land. Jamie didn't like flying and especially hated when planes circled. Her dark memories from the plane crash caused her to always take a tranquilizer before takeoff.

As they were disembarking in Atlanta, Jamie said, "I've been thinking about the Martin lawsuit. We're still going to have problems getting money on the case. If an arrest is made, it'll bring intense scrutiny to LAMPCO. The regulators might come in and audit LAMPCO. There'll be a media circus, and if that happens, other lawyers will file lawsuits and try to get a piece of the pie. LAMPCO might have to file bankruptcy to reorganize. If that happens, we won't get anything for the Martins. All of Dr. Elsworth's property was jointly owned, so since he was still legally married on the day of his death, all of his property passed to his wife. There are no assets in his estate to go after. We need to get what we can from LAMPCO and move on. We need to do it fast before anything becomes public."

Karen thought about it. It would be great to expose LAMPCO, but if they exposed LAMPCO, they might not get any settlement money for the Martin family. Bobby Martin only had a $10,000 life insurance policy, and Mrs. Martin was having a tough time financially since his death. Karen agreed it would be in her client's best interest to settle the case and not expose LAMPCO.

Doug and the local prosecutors could make arrests and go after the responsible people. It was not Karen's job to expose a murder; her job was to help Mrs. Martin get compensated for the wrong that was done to her husband. She wondered how Mrs. Martin would feel about not exposing the corruption at LAMPCO. Karen wanted to expose LAMPCO just like her hero Jay Hall had exposed the corrupt fertilizer companies. She mentally debated the best route for her and her client.

When Karen got home, she called Mrs. Martin and tried to explain everything that happened. She suggested trying to negotiate a settlement from LAMPCO based on what she knew.

Mrs. Martin said, "I don't really understand exactly everything you said. Nothin' they do is gonna bring Bobby back. I just want enough money so I can support myself and not be a burden on my children. I'll do whatever you think, Miss Senard."

Karen said she would do her best, hung up the phone, and thought about the situation. It was Karen's job to get a financial settlement for her client, who had lost her husband. The death occurred because of malpractice of a doctor, and/or the business practices of an insurance company. Since the insurance company was the only one with money, she'd go after them. The answer was simple. Her client would be happy to have enough money in the bank to support herself at the same standard of living she'd always lived. She only wanted to live by herself and be left alone.

Karen thought back to her first big high profile case. She

represented a Mrs. Cathleen Burgess, widowed by Dr. Ben Kern's malpractice. Mr. Burgess had gone in for routine surgery to remove a gallstone. Dr. Kern was an alcoholic and had been in rehab for three weeks before the surgery. He ended his treatment early, left rehab, and resumed his surgical practice. As he was operating on Mr. Burgess, he got a bad case of DTs, and his shaking hands caused him to accidentally cut Mr. Burgess' spleen. When he saw what he did, he accidentally dropped the scalpel and it cut an artery. Mr. Burgess died on the operating table within 20 minutes.

Dr. Kern hadn't paid his malpractice insurance premium, and coverage had lapsed at the time of Mr. Burgess' death. Dr. Kern had offered $100,000 of his own money to settle. Karen was convinced Dr. Kern was hiding assets, and told Ms. Burgess to go to trial. Karen presented her case to a jury two years later, and they returned a 2.2 million-dollar verdict.

The local media gave great press coverage to Karen. However, the next day Dr. Kern declared bankruptcy. Unfortunately, Dr. Kern had no hidden assets, and Mrs. Burgess collected nothing. Karen had advanced the costs of litigation. Two years of work and $52,000 of advanced costs later, Karen had nothing but an upset client. Dr. Kern continued his surgical practice after an extended stay in rehab.

Karen unpacked and checked her answering machine. There were two messages from Doug saying he missed her

already. Karen smiled and called him back. They talked for
an hour before she went to sleep. She slept deeply in spite
of some very naughty dreams about Doug. Karen woke up
early and got ready for work. As she drove to work, she
planned what to say to LAMPCO's lawyers. She didn't
know all of the pieces of the puzzles, but she knew enough
to talk tough and demand a settlement.

She arrived at work and looked at the Martin file, making last minute notes and thinking about the best strategy.
She finally settled on her plan. She waited until 9:00 a.m.
and called Don Welch at Prince and Wilson.

When Don Welch answered the phone and identified
himself, Karen said, "Good morning, Mr. Welch. I'm calling
about the Martin lawsuit against the late Dr. Elsworth and
LAMPCO. I've been doing some investigation on the case,
and I've found some amazing things. It seems the accident
that killed Dr. Elsworth was really a murder plot. The police
have found evidence of a bomb and traced it to a professional killer in Miami. They raided his apartment and seized
his computer. When it was examined, an e-mail from Al
Brognese, senior vice president of LAMPCO, was found. It
seems he was confirming a large amount of money was paid
by LAMPCO to a Swiss bank account owned by the professional killer. Unfortunately, the killer escaped."

Don Welch said lamely, "We deny all of this."

Karen continued. "That doesn't let LAMPCO off the

hook. I'm sure the accounting department at LAMPCO labeled the money for some type of business expense. I really doubt the IRS would consider hiring a hitman as a legitimate business expense. Therefore, it would be tax evasion. If we turn LAMPCO over to the IRS, we get a 10% finder's fee for your client's illegal activity. Then they are looking at an audit with interest and penalties. An aggressive prosecutor might even indict on tax evasion charges. Furthermore, I've done some research into the civil RICO statute. I think we could use the act of hiring a hitman to kill a material witness as further proof of the criminal conspiracy at LAMPCO. The jury would love that when awarding punitive damages. Think about it. Treble damages, punitive damages, and attorney fees added to an IRS audit and a criminal investigation of murder. Your clients are looking at a world-class fuckup! However, my clients realize that it won't help them if they put your clients into prison and bankruptcy court. Our original lawsuit was for 15 million against Dr. Elsworth. We'll settle for half of that—7.5 million—and agree to a non-disclosure agreement. We want payment within three business days, and this offer expires at five p.m. today."

There was silence on the other end of the line.

Karen asked, "Are you there?"

Don stammered quietly, "Yes, I'm here. I'll call you back by noon."

Chapter 27

Doug left the State Attorney's Office in a rage. The prosecutors said there was not enough evidence for the arrest of Al Brognese for murder and only circumstantial evidence of a bomb. There were no bomb fragments, detonation devices, or any eye witnesses to a bomb ever being placed on the boat. One witness saw Carlos in the water, in snorkeling gear, at the same dock the *Two Tongues* stopped at on the day of the explosion. The witness never saw a bomb or even saw Carlos swimming near the *Two Tongues*. It could've been an accidental explosion. They had to have proof beyond a reasonable doubt before they could go to a grand jury.

The raid on Carlos' apartment produced no evidence of a bomb, firearms, or books on explosives. The retrieved e-mail message of "*The money has been transferred*" means nothing because legitimate businessmen transfer money every day. Prosecutors told Doug they needed more evidence and witnesses. The only direct proof of Carlos being a hitman is a drug dealer awaiting sentencing that heard Carlos was a hitman. They said that's hearsay and can't be used as evidence. The mere fact that the drug dealer delivered a bag of cash to Carlos means nothing.

The prosecutors put salt in the wound by telling Doug he should've staked out Carlos' apartment and brought him in for questioning. They told Doug a confession by Carlos would allow them to make an arrest of Al Brognese. The prosecutors suggested bringing all of the officers of LAMP-CO in for questioning. One of them might get nervous and confess to their knowledge of the murder plan. If one of the officers confessed, they could make a plea bargain with him and agree to give him a reduced sentence if he testified against the others. The prosecutors said without a confession there was no way to make a murder charge stick in court. Doug was so angry he was seeing red because he knew it was difficult to get a confession on a murder case.

However, it was possible. He would have to plan every question. He would use every dirty trick and intimidation tactic he knew to get a confession. He was determined to get Sandy's killer. He went back to his office to arrange a flight to Atlanta and organize the required cooperation with the Atlanta police. He would need two marked units and some policemen to help him transport all of the officers of LAMPCO to the police station for questioning. It took him two hours to make all the arrangements. He decided to call Karen to tell her he was going to be in Atlanta for the night. He was looking forward to another passionate night with her.

Doug called Karen's office and reached her receptionist.

A few seconds later Karen picked up the phone and said, "What a great surprise. I was just thinking about you."

Doug felt himself blush, "Oh really, I think about you all the time. I've got to come to Atlanta and interview the officers at LAMPCO because the State Attorney's Office says we don't have enough evidence. I'm coming up tonight on the six o'clock Delta flight. Do you want to meet for dinner?"

Karen felt her stomach drop.

She said tentatively, "I have some good news. I called LAMPCO's lawyers this morning and told them about the evidence we found. I was able to negotiate a five million dollar settlement for my client."

Doug screamed, "You did what? You called LAMPCO's lawyers? They'll never talk now."

Karen asked with a cracking voice, "You can still bring them in for questioning, can't you?"

Doug yelled, "Of course, but it's no longer a surprise to them. Their lawyers will coach them to assert their Fifth Amendment rights to remain silent and not incriminate themselves."

Karen began to cry.

Between her tears she said, "I didn't know I would hurt your investigation. I was trying to help my client. She desperately needs the money."

Doug was so angry he could barely speak.

211

After a few moments of silence, he yelled sarcastically, "Money. You're so concerned about your client. You get 40% of that—two million dollars. You sacrificed justice for my friend for two million dollars."

Karen suddenly became angry, "I'm required to look out for the best interests of my client. I didn't intentionally try to hurt your investigation and you didn't tell me not to contact LAMPCO's lawyers."

Doug yelled back, "Any fool would know not to jeopardize an ongoing criminal investigation."

Karen pleaded, "I didn't know. I have an ethical duty to my client."

Doug screamed, "You can shove that ethical duty up your ass. You used me to get information and then took the money and ran. I never want to talk to you again. Have a good life."

Doug slammed the phone down. He looked around the squad room and saw dozens of silent faces staring at him. He stormed out of the Sheriff's office and headed home with a pounding headache.

Chapter 28

When Doug got home he changed into shorts and running shoes. He stretched and then began his daily run with his anger intensifying, but less channeled. He knew he was as much to blame as Karen for LAMPCO being warned. It's true he hadn't told Karen not to contact LAMPCO. He was so focused on his case, he forgot about her case and obligations to her clients.

Still, she was a smart woman and had to consider LAMPCO would be better prepared if she contacted them. He thought of the five million dollars that LAMPCO had used to purchase her silence. The justice system wasn't fair. Even if she hadn't contacted LAMPCO, it was possible Carlos alerted Al when his apartment was raided. If only Doug had been patient and staked out the condo to make sure Carlos was there when they raided it. His anger was making him light-headed.

Doug suddenly realized he was light-headed because he was sprinting as fast as he could go down the dirt road. He slowed down to catch his breath and unknowingly allowed the mosquitoes to catch their fleeing prey. The summer rains had produced a huge summer crop of the saltwater mosquitoes. Doug figured he had fed them enough as he swatted them off his arm, and increased his speed back to his house.

Doug decided to go to Atlanta to question LAMPCO'S officer's anyway. He knew it was a long shot, but he had to try. He made reservations for the flight and arranged to have local police support in Atlanta. He arrived in Atlanta on the 8:00 a.m. flight and was met at the airport by the Atlanta police. They had two squad cars and drove him to LAMPCO'S headquarters. Doug created a dramatic entrance when they entered the main administration building, asking for all LAMPCO officers.

Five minutes later Theodore Marion, Al Brognese, and Don Welch walked into the waiting room together.

Don said, "I am LAMPCO's attorney. Why are you here?"

Doug said loudly, "We're here to take all officers of LAMPCO downtown for questioning in a murder case."

Don said, "The only officers here are Mr. Marion and Mr. Brognese. All of the other officers of the corporation are at a seminar in Aspen. They are asserting their Fifth Amendment right to remain silent and don't wish to make a statement. If you don't have a warrant, please leave the building."

Doug stared at Theodore, who looked away and fidgeted back and forth on his feet. Doug switched his stare to Al and

214

saw him looking back at him with a smirk. Doug looked at Don and said, "We'll be back with arrest warrants. You can tell your clients to start getting ready for the electric chair."

It was a bluff, but it was Doug's last chance. He had secured a search warrant to tap all of the phones and internet computer lines for LAMPCO. Doug was hoping Theodore or Al would panic and use the phone or internet to make incriminating statements. Unfortunately, they were well coached by their lawyers and didn't panic. While in Atlanta, Doug thought about apologizing to Karen, but he couldn't bring himself to believe that she was totally innocent. After he left LAMPCO's headquarters, he reviewed all of the public records in the downtown courthouse for any other possible leads or witnesses. After two days in Atlanta, Doug returned to Ft. Myers certain that Al, Carlos, or LAMPCO would never be prosecuted.

* * * * *

The following week Doug caught up with his work on his other cases. On his first day off, he called Sandy's father and arranged to go to his house for dinner. Sandy's father was named Eugene but everyone called him Big Papa. Big Papa's wife had died three years before. Doug drove his Ford truck down the crushed shell and sand driveway as the sun was setting, and Big Papa was firing up his grill. It was

215

made out of a 55-gallon drum split in half. It was a large grill that took substantially more time to start and clean than a normal store-bought grill. However, it was worth the effort because he used aged hickory wood chips, which produced a fantastic taste. It was an event to cook out with Big Papa.

As Doug approached, Big Papa opened up a cooler sitting on the picnic table and grabbed two beers, tossing one to Doug. Big Papa put out his large, sun-spot covered right hand and said, "Damn, it's good to see ya, boy."

Doug shook his strong hand and said, "It's good to see you, Big Papa. I'm sorry I haven't been around like I shoulda since...since..."

Doug got choked up and had to clear his throat. Big Papa wiped a tear off his cheek and said, "It's been hard on all of us, Doug. It's O.K."

Doug regained his composure and sat down in the folding chair under the oak tree. He told Big Papa of the murder investigation and his conclusions. They had finished a 12-pack by the time Doug ended his story. Big Papa sat quietly and absorbed everything. He excused himself and went inside for the steaks. He came back out with a quart of Lord Calvert whiskey and two large cups of ice, along with the steaks.

He poured the whiskey, handed a cup to Doug, and said quietly, "My granddaddy always said to ask the Lord for guidance. He was a religious man and didn't mean any disrespect when he said that while drinking Lord Calvert. He didn't drink a lot but whenever he did, he drank this. The first drink I ever had in my life was when I was 12 and stayin' with him. I asked 'im if it was O.K. to drink, and he said Jesus drank wine in the Bible only because they hadn't invented Lord Calvert. I used to spend every summer with him on the boats fishing. He taught me so much."

Big Papa got up off his seat at the picnic table and moved the coals around and stirred up the fire. He took an exceptionally long drink and said, "A good pull on a drink sometimes makes a man see things differently. I remember when I was 14 and we couldn't afford to get me a bicycle. I told my granddaddy while we were drinkin' that it wasn't fair. He turned, looked at me seriously, and said, 'Boy, life only becomes fair when you realize it's unfair.'"

Big Papa looked at Doug as he took another long drink. Big Papa got up and put the steaks on the grill. As the steaks sizzled, they finished their first glass of whiskey and poured a second. Big Papa turned the steaks as they drank in silence. When the steaks were done, they went inside and Big Papa pulled a bowl of salad from the refrigerator to go with the steaks.

While eating, Big Papa asked, "I bet you didn't know Sandy had a will?"

Doug replied, "No, I didn't. I never thought about it."

Big Papa said, "He left the *Two Tongues* to you. His

will said the boat was bought with the prize money, so you two were partners. My probate lawyer, Mr. Jessell, says that means you're entitled to the insurance money from the boat. It was insured for $500,000, so you should have a nice nest egg."

Doug was taken aback. It's true the prize money bought the boat. The deal was Doug got 25% of the profits every year, but he hadn't thought about insurance money or wills. He looked up at Big Papa and said, "I don't want any of his money. You should have it."

Big Papa said, "No, I've got plenty of money to live on. It's his will, and he wanted you to have it."

Big Papa got up, staggered over to the counter, and poured them a third glass of whiskey. He brought the drinks back to the table and sat down. Slightly slurring his words, he said, "However, since it's your money, ya can do whatever ya want with it. You know, the Lord works in mysterious ways. It's not fair that insurance company got away with murder. It's not fair that hitman made money on my son's death. I realized a long time ago that life was unfair, and I think ya realize that, too."

Doug stared at Big Papa and nodded. "Life is very unfair."

Big Papa looked directly into Doug's eyes and asked, "Do you believe in the Bible?"

Doug answered instinctively, "Of course."

Big Papa's hands started quivering, tears flowed down his flushed cheeks and he said forcefully, "The Bible says an eye for an eye and a tooth for a tooth. The Lord has showed ya the proof of who killed Sandy. It's unfair that man's legal system didn't work. However, the Lord has provided resources to allow justice. Are you satisfied that life is unfair, or do you want to be the Archangel of the Lord and strike down the Philistines?"

Doug looked intently at Big Papa and said nothing as he felt a chill go through his body.

After the silence became deafening, Big Papa quietly said, "I'll go fix the spare bedroom. You don't need to be driving."

Doug agreed and stumbled to the bathroom.

Chapter 29

Doug woke up to the smell of fresh ground coffee and got out of bed. He walked down the hall to the kitchen and saw Big Papa mixing waffle mix.

Doug said, "Good mornin'. How are ya doing?"

Big Papa replied, "I'm feelin' great. It was good to talk last night, but you have to excuse me, though. Sometimes an old man says stupid things when he's been drinking."

"We all do," Doug laughed and continued. "You know the Germans have a saying, 'In the wine lies the truth.'"

Big Papa replied, "Thank goodness we weren't drinking wine."

Doug laughed and went to get a quick shower while Big Papa made waffles and bacon. After Doug finished breakfast, he said, "I need to go; I'm running late. We should do this again, I enjoyed it."

Big Papa replied, "Me too. Next month Mr. Jessell will distribute the money from Sandy's estate. I'll give you a call and maybe we can meet for lunch when I'm downtown."

Doug agreed and shook Big Papa's hand. As he was driving home, he couldn't forget the night before. The words

"Archangel of the Lord" kept ringing in his head. If Doug was to kill in retribution, was it a sin or was he administering punishment? He debated the pros and cons of being a vigilante. Doug had always believed in the legal system. At least, until Sandy's father explained it the way he did last night. Doug could feel an impulse to answer the call to arms by Big Papa. He told himself he was emotional and the impulse would go away with a good night's sleep.

Doug continued his daily work routine but couldn't stop thinking about Carlos and Al getting away with murder. Every night he had dreams of killing Carlos and Al. He kept thinking of Al's smirking face when he went to question him in Atlanta and imagined Carlos on a Caribbean island sipping drinks with umbrellas while two women rubbed suntan lotion on him. A month later Big Papa called and told him it was time to distribute the money. They agreed to meet at Mr. Jessell's office and then go to lunch.

His growing emotional need to avenge Sandy's death was beginning to overpower his natural disdain of vigilante justice. He thought of his friend at DEA, Mark Simion, and how he had watched him beat a drug dealer that was responsible for the death of Mark's friend and fellow officer. Doug couldn't condone his action, but even then he knew that every man had a breaking point. Mark was a good cop and Doug had to lie to support his claim of self-defense rather than trash his law enforcement career. He now understood

that emotion and how it consumed
subconscious thoughts.

Every night since dinner at Big Papa's, t.
killing Al and Carlos returned. The past week th.
come more vivid and detailed. His subconscious min.
planning their deaths every night in his dreams. He remembered Big Papa's words—"The Lord works in mysterious
ways." He wasn't sure if it was the Lord or not, but something was pushing him to kill and it went against everything
he had trained for as a policeman.

After meeting at Mr. Jessell's office, Doug and Big Papa
ate lunch at the Farmer's Market Restaurant and talked about
Big Papa's latest projects at his house. When they finished
eating they walked to the parking lot where they shook hands
to say goodbye.

Big Papa held Doug's hand and then covered it with his
other and said, "Doug, I know you'll do the right thing. If
you're not sure what that means, I have the answer for you.
Ask yourself, 'What would Sandy do if he were in your
shoes?'"

Doug nodded and said, "I'll talk to you later."

As Doug drove to SouthTrust Bank to deposit his
$500,000 check, he kept hearing Big Papa's words—"What
would Sandy do?" He remembered the bar fight at The Big
Still in Tallahassee and how Sandy had risked his life to save
him. Doug deposited the check and drove home listening to

223

＿ ₃y music. He changed into shorts and loaded his boat with beer, ice, and peanuts. He opened up his first beer as he cruised slowly down his canal and headed toward Boca Grande Pass.

Doug tried to put the revenge killings out of his mind, but he knew it was no use. He had never before felt such a compulsion. Whenever he tried to think of a reason not to kill them, he thought of the explosion. He couldn't live with himself if he didn't punish Sandy's killers. Doug didn't like what was happening to him, but he couldn't stop it.

He was on his third beer when he arrived in Boca Grande Pass. Over two months had passed since he saw Sandy, his crew, and the *Two Tongues* vaporized by the fiery explosion. He slowed his boat and turned the engine off, drifting with the outgoing tide. He remembered the noise and black smoke. He remembered Sandy's bloody shoe and all of the floating debris. He thought about all the flesh from the bodies that sunk into the water and was eaten by the fish. Doug closed his eyes and tried to force the thoughts from his mind.

It was August and the tarpon run was finished in the pass. There were four boats drifting the pass and bottom fishing for grouper and snapper. He tried to relax by eating peanuts between beers and watching the sailboats on the horizon. Doug drifted for an hour thinking about Sandy and his killers. The sound of thunder from an approaching storm

224

brought him back to reality. He started up his engine and headed back against the tide to Matlacha. He was ready to strike down the Philistines.

Chapter 30

When Doug arrived back in Matlacha, he tied his boat to the dock and went inside. He was amazed at how quickly he had organized his plan on the boat ride back from the pass. Once he made the final conscious decision to administer vigilante justice, his subconscious mind released all the detailed planning he had dreamed during the past month. His first step was to call the convicted drug dealer in Miami that showed him Carlos' condo, Martine Lunez, and arrange to meet. Martine was still on the streets doing undercover work for the DEA, trying to get his sentence cut. He had already received credit for showing Doug where Carlos had lived. He would be anxious to help.

Doug looked through his notes and found Martine's beeper number. Doug called, and he quickly returned the page. They made arrangements to meet in Miami the next night at the mezzanine lounge in the Marlin's stadium. Doug turned on his stereo to country music, unplugged his phone, and sat down at his kitchen table to diagram and organize his violent plans. He awoke the next morning rested and contented. On the way to work, he stopped at SouthTrust

Bank and rented a safety deposit box. He then waited in line to make a withdrawal.

The next available teller was a young redheaded woman with green stylish glasses and an oversized nametag telling the customers her name is "Judy." Doug handed her a savings withdrawal slip and said, "I would like all of it in hundreds. I'm going to put most of it in a safety deposit box here at the bank."

Judy looked at the withdrawal slip and saw that it was for $150,000. She coughed, smiled, and said, "I need to get my supervisor. Just a minute, please."

After meeting with the branch manager, Doug was told to come back after lunch and the cash would be available. He left to work on some other cases and returned after lunch. He took $25,000 in cash with him and put the remaining cash in his safety deposit box. As he left the bank, he couldn't help noticing all of the female tellers smiling at him.

Doug left work at four in the afternoon and drove over to Miami. When he walked into the lounge, the Marlins were leading the Dodger's 3 to 2 in the bottom of the fifth inning. He saw Martine at a table by the window overlooking the field. He sat down with a paper bag filled with money next to him. Martine gave him a quick recap of the game over a beer.

Doug said, "Do you remember Iceman?"

Martine replied, "Of course. He has fled Miami since

you searched his condo. No one knows where he has gone."

Doug said, "I need to find him because he killed a friend of mine. Just between you and me, I'm going to give you $10,000 cash to ask around and find what country he is hiding in. Once you find out which country he is in, I'll give you an additional $20,000. In case you're wondering, when my friend was killed I was a beneficiary in his will; that's why I have this money. I want to spend it to bring Carlos back to America for justice. I'm not going to tell anybody else about the money, so you don't have to pay taxes on it."

Doug doubted if Martine had ever paid taxes in his life. However, he figured Martine wouldn't talk as much if thought he could retain more money by keeping quiet. It was not illegal to give money for information, but he would rather the Miami DEA not know about his new wealth.

Martine said, "I will do everything I can to find Iceman for you. My family could use some money while I do my time."

Doug gave him his card with all of his numbers and the bag of money. Doug left him and drove to the Holiday Inn near the Miami Airport. He paid cash for a room and relaxed for the night. The next morning he checked out and drove to the airport. He paid cash for a round trip ticket to Atlanta. Before he left, he called his office and told them he was sick.

Once in Atlanta, he hailed a taxi and told the driver to take him downtown to the Old South Detective Agency.

Doug had researched the agency on the internet and was satisfied they were qualified. On the taxi ride there, he opened up his old, faded-blue duffel bag and pulled out an old Atlanta Braves hat. He asked the driver about the previous night's Braves game and listened to a detailed description until they arrived at the Old South Detective Agency. He paid and tipped the taxi driver $50 for him to stay for a return trip.

As Doug was walking down the street with his duffel bag, he pulled out a pair of old black horn-rimmed glasses with non-prescription glass lenses from his pocket. It was not a great disguise, but when he looked at his reflection walking past a window, he thought he looked like a skinny Billy Carter. He went inside and met the owner, Stan Wasserman.

Doug sat down at Stan's old metal desk and said, "I would like to hire your agency to track a person for me. I think my wife is having an affair with him. I want to know his daily schedule and what his habits are. I want you to track him 24 hours a day, 7 days a week for the next three weeks. I want to serve him with legal papers and I want to do it when it will embarrass him the most.

"His name is Al Brognese and he works for LAMPCO insurance. I have a list here with his address, social security number, and birthdate."

Stan smiled and said, "We can do it for you, but it's going to be expensive. I need $2,500 for each week plus expenses."

Doug opened up his duffel bag, pulled out $10,000 in cash and said, "Here is ten thousand. I'll come back in three or four weeks for the information and bring another ten. I want this to be a first class job."

Stan looked in wonder at Doug and said, "You got it, buddy. What's your name? How do I contact you?"

Doug said, "My name is Jack. I'll contact you when I come back in three or four weeks with the rest of the money."

Doug left Stan with the cash, certain that he would soon know all about Al's habits. He returned to his taxi and took off his hat and fake glasses. The taxi driver gladly drove his generous fare back to the airport.

He flew back to Miami and then drove to Ft. Myers. The next morning he was back at work, where he continued working on his other cases for the next two weeks waiting for a call. Driving home one afternoon, he received a page from Martine. When he got home he called Martine at a new number.

Martine answered, "Hello, amigo. How are you tonight? I've been drinking some sangria with my wife because we were celebrating finding Carlos. I still get the extra $20,000, don't I?"

Doug said, "If you know what country, yes, you'll get the extra $20,000."

Martin said, "Colombia. I asked and bribed many people. I finally talked to a mate that was on the ship when he escaped Miami. Iceman left the ship with his luggage in Barranquilla, Colombia. That's all I know."

Doug said, "I'll be in Miami tomorrow. I'll page you and give you the money."

The next morning Doug went to the Sheriff's Department and told his supervisor he was going to take a 30 day vacation. He had over 70 vacation days saved up over the past eight years. Doug's supervisor agreed; he had been trying to get Doug to take time off since Sandy's death because he seemed very preoccupied and distant.

When he left his supervisor's office, he stopped by the inventory room and told the clerk, "I was checking the inventory in my detective car and realized I don't have that new gadget for stopping high speed chases."

The clerk answered, "I'm not sure what you mean."

Doug said, "You know those things that look like long vinyl belts that have spikes that stick up. You unroll them across the road before a bad guy drives by and the spikes puncture his tires. The tires deflate, and he has to stop because he can't keep driving on the tire rims."

The clerk said, "Oh, you mean the spike strip."

She checked one out and gave it to Doug. He took it with him and put it in his truck. He drove home, packed, loaded his truck, and headed to SouthTrust Bank. All the

232

tellers smiled at him as he walked by to the safety deposit area. He put $100,000 cash in his duffel bag and returned his box with the remaining cash.

On the way to Miami, Doug listened to the Spanish radio stations trying to recall the two years of Spanish he had taken at Florida State. When he arrived in Miami, he paged Martine and met him at the Greyhound Bus Station, where he gave him $20,000. He went to the airport and paid cash for a ticket to Barranquilla. While Doug waited for the flight, he had lunch and watched all the people hurrying through the corridors. Doug was surprised at how easily he had adapted from being a policeman to an assassin. The jobs were actually very similar: research your target, track him down, and then finish the job. In the past that had meant making an arrest, but now it meant killing your target. Whenever he felt guilty he thought of Big Papa asking him, "What would Sandy do?"

The flight to Barranquilla was comfortable and he passed through customs without a problem. He hailed a taxi and asked to be taken to the Hotel of the Americas. His search on the internet for a hotel that was expensive and catered to foreigners had turned up three hotels that fit this category, but the Hotel of the Americas had the best fishing fleet. He decided his cover was going to be an American accountant on a fishing trip.

He checked into the hotel and rented a safe. He took

$12,000 from his duffel bag and put the rest in his safe. He sat on a couch in the lobby and smoked a Cuban cigar while watching the four bellhops help move the luggage of the new arrivals. He watched the body language of the bellhops and how they interacted with strangers. After an hour, he approached a short bellhop with a continuous smile.

Doug said, "I'm having problems unloading my luggage, could you help me?"

"Of course, señor. My name is Edwardo, but my friends call me Eddie. Where is your luggage?"

Doug replied, "It's down in the garage. Walk with me."

Doug and Eddie walked out the side entrance and into the garage while making small talk about the weather. Once they turned the corner to the lower level, Doug said, "I have a friend that stayed here at this hotel and told me you were the source of good information. I don't have a problem with my luggage;I just wanted to talk to you away from your supervisor."

Eddie nodded anxiously. "Yes, señor."

"Here is five hundred dollars. I need you to tell me the name of a good private investigator. I need to find someone in Colombia that doesn't want to be found."

Eddie looked at the money, took it, and then said to Doug, "That is easy, señor. Is there anything else you want?"

Doug replied, "I might want something else in the future,

but first I need to see if you direct me to the best investigator in the country."

Eddie said, "Come with me and I will take you to a trusted friend of mine who drives a cab. He will take you downtown to their office."

Eddie and Doug walked back into the lobby and out the main entrance to where the cabs were waiting. Eddie waived to a light-skinned Hispanic man driving a beat-up green taxi. Eddie approached and said, "Roberto, how are you my friend? I have an important man you must drive downtown. Mr. Doug, this is Roberto. He is the most talented driver in the city."

Doug shook hands with Roberto, feeling his moist palms, and smelling his bad breath. Roberto said, "I'm at you service, señor. Where would you like to go?"

Eddie said, "Take him to Señor Perez's business on Second Street. It is the light blue building by the square."

As they drove downtown, Roberto entertained Doug with his tales of the wild nightlife downtown. When they arrived, Doug handed him a hundred-dollar bill and asked him to wait for him. Doug exited the cab and walked into an old storefront that said "Perez Communications." Once inside the door, it was a perfectly modern building that would have been Grade "A" office space in the U.S. The air was cool and the overhead lights were bright. There was a waiting room with a glass wall that showed the main room, which was filled with small desks and large computers. People were scurrying back and forth between the desks and the computers, and everyone was dressed professionally.

The receptionist finished taking the incoming call and asked in perfect English, "May I help you?"

Doug told her he was interested in hiring the firm to find a person. She told him to have a seat and someone would help him. After five minutes passed, the door opened and a slight man with graying hair and reading glasses walked out and greeted Doug.

"I am Mr. Perez. How may I help you?"

"My name is Doug Shearer, and I'm looking for someone. He has come to Colombia to hide. I have his picture, but he may have changed his appearance. I do know he arrived in Barranquilla approximately two months ago," Doug said as he handed him an enlarged picture of Carlos' fake driver's license and continued, "I'll give you $10,000 now. Once he is found, I want to know his habits and daily routine. After he has been observed for a week, I'll pay you an additional $30,000."

Mr. Perez asked, "All you want me to do is find him. You don't want me to do anything to him?"

Doug said, "That's right. I'll deal with him when you find him.

Mr. Perez smiled and said, "It's a deal. I will contact you at your hotel when I have located this man."

Doug returned to his hotel and went to the pool bar to get drunk to help establish his cover. He was very generous buying drinks for everyone and quickly made friends. Over the next week, he chartered fishing boats during the day and partied every night. He thought to himself, this is the best undercover work I've ever done.

Twelve days later, he got the call he had been waiting for. Doug went to the hotel safe, filled his duffel bag and headed downtown in Roberto's taxi. He walked inside the storefront and he was escorted back to Mr. Perez's office.

Mr. Perez said, "Your friend was very well hidden and had bribed many people. He may be Hispanic, but the locals don't like Spanish-Americans. I had to remind some of my people of this fact. Nevertheless, I have found him," Mr. Perez paused. "You have the money with you?"

Doug opened up the duffel bag and dumped the money on the table. Mr. Perez counted the money and then said, "He is in Calamar. It is a small town, approximately 60 miles south of Barranquilla. I have prepared a report giving you his daily schedule and habits."

Doug thanked Mr. Perez and walked out to Roberto's waiting taxi. Doug had given Roberto $100 every time they took a trip, and he could tell Roberto would do just about anything for an America dollar. On the way back to the hotel, Doug explained, "I'm going to take a trip tomorrow to find a friend, but I've been told it's dangerous for Americans

237

outside of Barranquilla. I want you to buy a handgun for me so I'll have protection. I'll give you $500 to buy a handgun and ammunition for me."

Roberto said, "That is no problem, señor. Do you need anything else? Maybe some good powder for a party?"

Doug said, "Actually, bring me some of your clothes to wear. I want to blend in."

He gave Roberto the money, and they agreed to meet at noon the next day in front of the hotel. He went back to his room to digest the report from Mr. Perez. It seemed Carlos was going by the name Benjamin Acosta, living in a modest house on the outside of town. He was driving a late model BMW and was considered a rich man. Carlos had alienated the locals by dating many of their women. He had a maid come in every morning and clean, and every night he drove to a restaurant for dinner by himself. Some nights he called for women to come over, other nights he read.

After studying the report, Doug went to the bathroom and looked in the mirror. He hadn't shaved since arriving in Colombia. He had been outside every day and developed a deep tan. The scruffy beard and tan combined with a hat and local clothes would make him blend in better.

The next morning Doug went down to the pool for a morning swim to clear his mind. After a small breakfast at poolside, he returned to his room and dressed. He stopped and got some cash from the safe. Roberto pulled up to the hotel at five before noon.

Doug got in and asked, "Do you have everything?"

Roberto replied, "Of course. I have a .38 caliber with six bullets and I brought you my clothes I wore yesterday."

Doug told him to stop at a store for supplies. Roberto waited in the taxi while Doug purchased 20 feet of thin rope, electrical tape, gloves, a hunting knife, and a plastic bottle of Evian water. He went to the store's bathroom and changed into Roberto's smelly clothes.

Once they arrived in Calamar, Doug said, "I have a favor to ask. I would like you to purchase a used motorcycle for me. I will use it here in my travels. When I get back to Barranquilla, I'll give you the motorcycle."

Roberto said, "Whatever your wish. It's not smart for a Gringo to be riding a motorcycle in the country with a gun."

Roberto pulled into a market area, and Doug gave him $1,000 for the motorcycle. Doug stayed in the taxi and Roberto returned in thirty minutes with a beat-up Honda. Doug drove the taxi to the woods outside of town with Roberto following on the motorcycle. They pulled off the bumpy dirt road and stopped.

Doug said, "I'll go by myself from here. I want to surprise my friend. I'll be back in Barranquilla tomorrow. Here is $500 for your time."

Roberto looked warily at Doug and said, "Are you sure you want to do this? This country can be very dangerous."

239

Doug assured him he would be all right, and Roberto left. He rode his Honda deeper into the woods and waited for dark. The report said Carlos left his house between 7:00 and 7:30 every night and returned around 10:00 p.m. At 8:00 p.m., Doug started up the motorcycle and headed into town. He had pictures of the house in the report and a detailed map. He drove past the house to make sure there were no lights on. He saw none and turned around. Satisfied Carlos was gone, he turned off his headlight as he drove up the driveway. He parked his Honda behind the house and surveyed the area. There was vacant land behind the house, and it was dark. There was one neighbor to the north side and a pond on the south side.

Doug unpacked his duffel bag. He drank the water from the Evian bottle and then used the hunting knife to cut the top off the plastic bottle. He loaded his gun and then put the barrel through the hole in the plastic bottle. He used the electrical tape to wrap and secure the plastic bottle over the barrel and had a makeshift silencer. He cut the rope into four equal pieces and put them in his duffel bag, along with the hunting knife and tape. He put on the gloves and waited for Carlos.

After the longest hour of Doug's life, he heard the electric garage opener activate and saw the headlights light up the backyard. He waited until he heard Carlos put the car in park in the garage. He walked from behind the house and into the garage with his gun pointed at Carlos.

As Carlos opened his door, Doug said, "Exit your vehicle slowly, this is a robbery. If you cooperate, I won't kill you."

He didn't want to risk a struggle in the garage or the house where he would have to shoot Carlos randomly. He had a plan.

Carlos raised his hands and said, "Don't shoot. I will show you where my jewelry is located."

Doug said, "Walk over to the wall and push the button that closes the garage."

Carlos complied. Doug told him to go inside and turn on the stereo. Carlos did as ordered. Doug told him to go to his bedroom and strip because he wanted to make sure there were no hidden weapons. Doug watched carefully as he stripped completely naked.

Doug said, "Sit on your bed."

Doug waited until Carlos sat on his bed and then slowly walked toward him as he said, "You know that boat you blew up in Boca Grande Pass? My friend was the Captain."

Doug waited until the fear registered in Carlos' eyes, fired twice, and watched blood explode from his chest. Doug moved quickly according to his plan. He pulled Carlos to the middle of his bed. He pulled out the hunting knife, grabbed Carlos' penis and sliced it off. More blood flowed. He opened Carlos' mouth and put his shriveled, bloody penis on his tongue. When his mouth closed, the severed end was protruding from his lips. He quickly pulled out the four pieces of rope and tied Carlos' limbs spread-eagle to the bedposts.

Doug looked at the crime scene, and it definitely looked like a crime of passion. It looked like a jealous boyfriend of one of Carlos' women had decided to torture and kill him. He had tied Carlos naked to his bedposts and then cut off his penis. The jealous boyfriend watched him bleed and suffer. Before he left, he put two bullets in the heart to make sure he was dead and then carefully placed the playboy's penis in his mouth.

According to Mr. Perez's report, there were many jealous boyfriends, and the local police would have a lot of suspects to question. Meanwhile, the visiting American accountant could leave Colombia after his fishing vacation and not draw attention.

Chapter 31

Doug returned to Miami, drove back to Ft. Myers, checked his house for messages and spent the night. He rested well knowing one Philistine was slain.

The next morning he shaved his beard, packed and drove down to SouthTrust Bank. He took another $15,000 from his safety deposit box and put it in his duffel bag with the remaining cash from Colombia. He then began the 12-hour drive up Interstate 75 to Atlanta, paying cash for all gas and food. Driving through Atlanta, he involuntarily thought of Karen, but wouldn't allow himself to forgive her. He paid cash for a room at Motel 6 off of Interstate 85 in North Atlanta.

The next morning he drove into downtown Atlanta and parked around the corner from the Old South Detective Agency. He put on his old black horn-rimmed glasses and Atlanta Braves cap as he walked down the street with his duffel bag.

As soon as he walked in the front door, Stan Wasserman rushed forward to meet him saying, "Jack, how are you? I was wondering if you were coming back. It's been almost four weeks."

Doug asked, "Do you have what I requested?"

Stan replied, "Of course, Jack. It's a very detailed report, and I wanted it to be perfect since you were paying such a premium."

Stan reinforced Doug's belief that greed was a universal motivation. He pulled out $10,000 and gave it to Stan, certain that he had already spent the money. Doug left and walked down the street two blocks before he circled back around toward his car. He double-backed twice to make sure he wasn't being followed by anyone associated with Stan that might be curious about his real identity.

Satisfied no one was following him, he drove back to the Motel 6 to read the report. It appeared Al Brognese was a very busy man. He left his house in Lawrenceville at 6:30 a.m. every Monday and commuted an hour to LAMPCO'S offices in downtown Atlanta. Every morning he ate breakfast and read the paper at a small restaurant across the street from his building. Every Monday, Wednesday, and Friday he would go to the gym at 3:00 p.m. and walk on the Stairmaster for 30 minutes. Every Tuesday and Thursday at 3:00 p.m. he would go to the Cheetah III strip club until 5:00 p.m. Every weeknight but Thursday, he would be home by 6:30 p.m.

On Thursdays, he played in a poker game at the Idle Hour Country Club located on the shore of Lake Lanier from 7:00 p.m. until midnight. He made the 45-minute drive home and begin his normal routine at 6:30 a.m. the next morning. On weekends he stayed home, except for Saturday night. It appeared Mrs. Brognese was in charge on Saturday night. They always went out to dinner and then to a party or to a movie.

It was Tuesday afternoon at 2:00 p.m,. and Doug decided to check the accuracy of the report. He called, got directions to the Cheetah III, and drove by at 2:30 p.m. He pulled into a Burger King across the street from the Cheetah III and ordered lunch. After lunch, he read the newspaper sitting by a window that looked across the street and waited for Al's black Mercedes sedan.

At 3:05 p.m. Al pulled into the parking lot of the Cheetah III. Doug was satisfied and walked to his truck, where he checked a local map. He decided to drive out to the Idle Hour Country Club and see the area. Once he got outside of the congested afternoon traffic on the perimeter of Atlanta, Doug enjoyed the beauty of the countryside.

Doug had lived in Florida all his life and had driven on its flat roads, so he loved driving through the hills and valleys of Georgia. He arrived at the Idle Hour at 5:00 p.m., where he found over 100 cars in the parking lot. The well-manicured lawn was protected by a guardhouse at the gated entrance, and the two-story main building looked like an old plantation home. He drove past to see if there were other businesses out in the rural area and discovered a country diner, a few bed-and-breakfasts on the main road, but mainly large residential homes overlooking the lake.

Doug pulled over on the curb and studied the map for possible routes from the Idle Hour to Al's home. There was only one direct route, a two-lane road that didn't go through any towns. He turned his truck around, went back to an intersection, and turned south onto State Road 414. It was a 45-minute drive to Al's house on the winding two-lane road, completely lined with pine trees, except for the creeks and farms.

After completing the drive, Doug turned around and drove back toward the Idle Hour. He stopped at the few roads that intersected with S.R. 414. After arriving back at the Idle Hour, he drove to the country diner and had dinner. By the time he finished dinner, it was dark and he again made the drive from the Idle Hour to Al's house. There were very few houses along the road and even fewer cars. Satisfied with his scouting trip, he returned to his motel.

The next morning Doug went to The Sports Authority and paid cash for night vision binoculars, 30 feet of thin rope, a hunting knife, three 5-gallon plastic gas cans, a tarp, and gloves. He used cash so his credit card purchases couldn't be traced to prove he was in Atlanta when Al died. He drove back out to S.R. 414 and down the side road that was best suitable for his purposes. He parked his truck and

246

walked around the area until satisfied with his plan. That afternoon he went to watch the Braves play a double-header. Later that night he stopped at a construction site and stole a blinking detour sign. He wrapped it in the tarp and hid it in the back of his truck.

The next morning Doug drove to Stone Mountain to admire the sites and kill time until Al's poker game later that night. After a day of playing tourist, he stopped at the liquor store and got a pint of Lord Calvert. He had dinner and saw a 7:00 p.m. movie at the Peachtree Mall. He left the mall and filled up his truck and the three cans with gas. He arrived at the intersection of S.R. 414 and County Line Road at 10:00 p.m. He pulled his truck off S.R. 414 onto the shoulder of County Line Road. He pulled out the rope and cut it into one section that was twenty feet and two five-foot sections. He left the rope and knife in the front seat of his truck next to the spike strip that had been in his truck for almost a month. He got out his night vision binoculars and climbed a hill so he could see Al's car on the winding road. He had timed the drive from the spot he would see Al's car on the nearest hill to the intersection. He had approximately two minutes before Al's car would reach the intersection.

Doug waited on the hill, watching for Al's car. Twenty minutes after midnight, Doug saw Al's car speeding down the deserted road. He ran down the hill and pulled the blinking detour sign out of his truck bed. He placed it across

247

S.R. 414 with the arrow pointing down County Line Road. He jumped in his truck and drove just past the first turn of County Line Road. He got out the spike strip and laid it across the road with its spikes shining in the moonlight. He drove 100 yards down the road and turned around facing the spike strip with his bright lights on.

He waited about 15 seconds before Al came racing around the corner and over the spikes. The air exploded out of the punctured tires, and the car started to slide. The Mercedes finally slid to a stop on the edge of the road, about 25 feet from Doug's truck. Doug drove up to the Mercedes and parked.

As he got out of his truck, he grabbed the hunting knife and rope. Al got out of his Mercedes screaming, "What the hell happened? Did you see that?"

Doug approached Al and said, "Yes, I saw it. Now sit down on the ground or I'll slit your throat."

Al obeyed and sat down. Doug took one of the shorter ropes and tied Al's hands together in front of him. He then took the second piece and tied Al's ankles together. He left Al on the ground while he turned the Mercedes so it was facing the edge that sloped down the hill. He left the car running, dragged Al to it and put him back in the driver's seat and fastened the seatbelt. He took the long piece of rope and tied Al to the driver's seat.

Al yelled, "What the hell are you doing? Are you

crazy?"

Doug said nothing as he got the three cans of gas. He put one in the back seat and one in the front passenger seat. Al stopped yelling profanities when Doug asked quietly, "You don't recognize me, do you? I'm the cop from Ft. Myers investigating the murders of the people on the boat that exploded. My best friend was the Captain."

Doug opened the bottle of Lord Calvert and took a drink. He stuffed his handkerchief into the top of the bottle and set it down on the ground. Doug opened the third can of gas and poured it all over the inside of the car and on Al as he was screaming for help. He reached in through the open driver's door and put the gearshift in drive. The car's rims started to turn, moving it toward the edge of the slope. Al quickly pulled his roped feet up and pressed them hard on the brake.

Doug picked up the Lord Calvert bottle, now converted to a Molotov cocktail and lit the handkerchief. Al screamed in agony as Doug threw the burning Molotov cocktail at his chest. Doug stepped away as flames covered Al and the inside of the car. It wasn't three seconds before Al's body started going into convulsions and the brake was released. The burning car crept slowly to the edge of the road, and then gravity took over as it rolled down the hill. The car bounced off of small pine trees and crashed into a granite boulder at the bottom of the hill by a creek bed. Ten seconds

249

later the gas cans exploded into a fireball.

Doug quickly retreated to his truck and drove back to the spike strip across the road. He picked it up and threw it in the back of his truck. He then drove to the intersection, picked up the detour sign, and covered it with the tarp in the back of the truck. He drove back towards Atlanta, dropping the detour sign at the first construction site.

Driving south on Interstate 75, he thought of how the accident scene would look. There would be skid marks and small pieces of tire on the road. The police would think Al had a blowout of his tires and lost control. The fire would destroy the ropes and melt most of the tires. Any remaining pieces of tire would be consistent with a blown tire. Their investigation would show that Al was drinking during his poker game. A careful examination of the wreck scene would show a broken Lord Calvert bottle. In fact, he was so impaired he made a wrong turn off his normal route home. The newspaper would report another sad victim of drinking and driving.

He thought of what he was going to do with the remaining money he had inherited from Sandy. He decided to keep $15,000 for a new engine for his boat and the rest he would use to set up a scholarship in Sandy's name. The scholarship would benefit the children of Boca Grande fishing guides wanting to attend college. Doug was sure that would make Big Papa proud.

Chapter 32

Karen walked into her office on a cool and windy Saturday morning in the fall. She wasn't surprised to see Jamie already at work.

Jamie looked up and asked, "Good morning, boss. Did you go out last night?"

Karen poured a cup of coffee and said, "No. I stayed at home and watched videos. I watched *Casablanca* and *An Officer and a Gentleman*. I used up a half box of Kleenexes."

Jamie asked, "Have you heard from Doug?"

"No. He hasn't returned my phone calls. It's been three months. He's not going to forgive me," Karen sighed.

"Doug is hard-headed," Jamie observed. "You're not going to change him. The only thing you can change on another person is their diapers."

Karen laughed and said, "I guess you're right." She took a sip of coffee and said, "There haven't been any arrests made of LAMPCO officers or Carlos."

Jamie said, "Yesterday, in the Wall Street Journal, there was a big article about LAMPCO being sold. National

Medical Plans, Inc. bought them out at $215 a share. The original investors got rich on the buyout."

Karen said, "I talked to Mrs. Martin this week. She put down new carpet and installed a new roof. I told her that with the settlement money she could buy a new house. She said she'd never leave that house; it was home, and she was happy there."

Jamie said, "It looks like those crooks got away with it. Well, except for Al Brognese. The newspaper said he died in a one-car accident a couple of weeks ago. They said he had been drinking when a tire blew out and he lost control. I guess the Lord gave us a little justice."

Karen remembered, "I saw Fast Eddie the other day at the courthouse. He had on a new yellow silk suit, with his hair slicked back, and he looked like a pimp. I tried to talk to him, but he turned and walked away."

"I've got a surprise for you," Jamie said, changing the subject.

"What do you mean?" Karen frowned, doubting it could possibly be good news.

Jamie said, "You've been depressed ever since your breakup with Doug. You don't go out and you look sad all the time, so I decided to try to put a little spice in your life."

Karen eyes widened and she groaned, "Oh, no, not another blind date. You know how I hate them."

Jamie explained, "Well, it's not exactly a blind date. I

was bored the other night and got on the Internet. I started looking up old friends on the databases and found a lot of people. I remembered the college sweetheart you always talk about, Alan Leopart. I decided to look him up and was able to find a lot of information about him. His wife died last year and he has two daughters, ages 10 and 7. He is living and working in Atlanta. I did a little detective work, and found out his boss is friends with one of my friends. So, I arranged for Alan and his boss to be at the bar at the Ritz-Carlton tonight at 6:00 p.m. and Alan doesn't know you'll be there."

Karen looked at Jamie in amazement and said, "I can't believe you did this. What were you thinking?"

Jamie answered, "Oh, come on. I've listened to you complain for the last eight years that no one has ever treated you as good as Alan. It can't hurt to see him. All the etiquette books say a widower should wait a year before he starts dating again. You should jump in there."

Karen was overwhelmed. "I can't believe you did this. How do you know that I don't have plans for tonight?"

Jamie smiled and said, "I guessed. Besides, if I told you earlier, you would have worried about it. You can go home at noon, take a nice long bath, take your time getting ready, and plan for a fun reunion."

Karen's mind swirled with old memories. She couldn't believe that Jamie would do something like this, but it would be nice to see Alan. The chances of them getting back to-gether were pretty remote though. But if they did, it would be different this time. Karen was financially secure and was ready to settle down. It would be fun to be around two girls. And maybe, just maybe, she could have a daughter of her own, before it was too late.

Her mind was racing with conflicting thoughts as she smiled at Jamie and said, "You like to see me like this, don't you?"

Jamie said sadly, "Yes. At least one of us should have a life."

Karen left the office to shop for a new outfit. She really wanted to look her best, so she called her salon and made an afternoon appointment for a facial and manicure. After the appointment, she went home and sat in her Jacuzzi for an hour.

She was relaxed and confident as she dressed. She kept thinking back to the good times she had with Alan in college. When she looked in the mirror, her heartfelt smile made her look 10 years younger. Karen met Jamie at the Ritz-Carlton at 5:45 p.m. and they each ordered a glass of red wine.

Jamie said, "Boss, you look gorgeous. He'll be begging you to go out with him."

Karen said, "I don't know. It's been 18 years since I've seen him. I hope I haven't aged that much."

Karen and Jamie were sitting at a table when Alan

walked into the bar. Karen couldn't take her eyes off him. He hadn't aged a bit or put on any weight. There was no baldness or gray hair, and Karen felt her heart beating up in her throat. Karen walked toward Alan, and when he saw her he smiled, walked over to her, and gave her a big hug. Karen thought it was a magical moment and too good to be true as she felt blood rush to her extremities.

Alan held her at arm's length and said, "How are you? You look great."

Karen replied, "I'm doing fine. What about you? How are you doing?"

"I'm having a tough time," Alan confided. "My wife committed suicide almost a year ago, and my daughters and I have been in therapy since then. I have a lot of guilty feelings."

Karen said, "That's terrible. But you shouldn't feel guilty; it was her decision."

Alan looked at her sadly and explained, "You don't understand. I started talking in my sleep after we got married. She said I always called out your name in my sleep. I went to counseling, but apparently I kept saying your name in my sleep. My wife got treatment for depression, but it didn't work. Her suicide note said, 'I can't compete with Karen.'"

Karen's face turned fluorescent white. She didn't know what to say and suddenly felt very dirty.

Alan said, "I'm sorry, it's not your fault. But I feel

guilty even talking to you. My daughters would be crushed; they're my whole life now."

Karen had to sit down because she felt like she'd been run over by a truck. Alan looked at her, and a tear rolled down his left cheek.

Alan said, "I need to go. Good luck with your law practice."

As she watched Alan walk away, she took a deep breath and walked to the bar. She ordered a tequila shot and downed it with one swallow. She felt it burn as it slid down her throat and into her stomach. Once again, Karen was reminded the taste of success was often bitter.

About the Author

John D. Mills is a fifth generation native of Ft. Myers, Florida. He grew up fishing the waters of Pine Island Sound and it's still his favorite hobby. He graduated from Mercer University in Macon, Georgia with a BBA in Finance and worked for Lee County Bank in Ft. Myers for five months. He returned to Macon and graduated from Mercer's law school in 1989.

He started his legal career as a prosecutor for the State Attorney's Office in Ft. Myers. In 1990, he began his private practice concentrating in Divorce and Criminal Defense.

Made in the USA
Columbia, SC
29 March 2019